DUELING DADDIES

LEE SAVINO

FREE BOOK

Royally Bad

Billionaire. Playboy. Prince. My new boss.

—>Bossy bad boy billionaire

—> Heroine who refuses to be intimidated

—>He's next in line for the throne...if he can keep his dick in his pants and name out of the tabloids

—> She's not falling in love with her arrogant, annoying, sex god boss. Nope. No way.

Grab it for free! https://BookHip.com/MQTSGH

HER DUELING DADDIES

Two daddies are better than one...

I'm caught between two dominant daddies--best friends who compete at everything. Both Bear and Sawyer have muscles for days but they want to know who's better in bed. And they want *me* to judge.

Their game, their rules, but I can play along. They call the shots, in and out of bed, and disobedience has delicious consequences.

As the final round approaches and the stakes are raised, I'm hoping this isn't just a game.

I'm falling, fast, and I don't think I can choose.

They're both playing to win. But which one's playing for keeps?

CHAPTER 1

"And that is why I'm never, ever sleeping with a guy again," I announce and set my glass very carefully back on the bar, which is blurry and not quite level. I frown. The bar was level when I came in.

"Never?" The bartender leans close. He's a surfer dude with tanned skin, shoulder-length blond hair and sparkling blue eyes.

Shame I'm no longer dating.

"Never ever," I confirm.

"Too bad," a voice rumbles high above my head.

I look up. And up. And up some more. Towering over me is the biggest guy I've ever seen, complete with a muscle shirt stretched over impressive pecs. I couldn't fit both hands around one of his taut biceps.

"Whoa," I breathe. I swing my head back and forth between him and the hot bartender. One looks like a swimsuit model and the other belongs on the cover of a weightlifting men's magazine. Why the heck couldn't they have shown up an hour earlier? Before I swore off men forever.

"A bottle of water for the lady," the newcomer rumbles.

The bar is dimly lit, the flickering light from a few TVs washing over the big guy's face.

"You're tall," I tell him.

He arches an eyebrow at me. I take a moment to marvel at his perfect lips and jawline.

"You are also..." I think for a moment, "very large."

His face splits into a grin.

"Anyway, as I was saying," I raise a finger to make my point. "Sleeping with guys is overrated."

"Sounds like you haven't been with the right guy," Hottie Bartender says. He and Mr. Men's Magazine exchange glances.

"Nope," I announce cheerfully. "But it's okay. I'm getting a vibrator. A big one." I set my hands apart to show the length. "Battery operated boyfriend. B-O-B. Big... Bob."

"You think Bob will do the job?" the bartender asks.

I nod vigorously.

He leans closer, blue eyes flashing mischief. "You should come back and give me a full report."

"Why?" I cock my head. "Are you shopping for one?"

The bartender turns his head to hide his laugh. "This is better than television," he says to the newcomer, who agrees. Most everyone in here is playing pool or watching some big sports game, but these guys are totally focused on me.

I rest my hands on the bar, warm all over from the praise.

The bartender hands a bottle of water to the big guy, who opens it and offers it to me. Big guy is still grinning. I can just hear him thinking how cute I am. His eyes amble over me as I gulp down some water, and I almost choke.

"Easy, baby," he murmurs, his voice rumbling against my ear. Shiver. His biceps are practically the size of my head. I imagine us horizontal, me sliding up the hard plane of his body, my softness molding to his muscles.

No. Nope. Not happening.

"My vow will not be broken!" I try to slam my hand down on the bar. Something sloshes over my hand. I stare at the now half empty water bottle that I forgot I was holding. "Oops."

"No worries." Hottie Bartender mops up with a towel and the big guy leans in close.

"Why not, baby?"

Baby. I like that. What was I saying again?

"Guys suck. They want you to suck. But they never give you an—" I hiccup. "—anything in return." I know this from personal experience. Jerry wasn't winning any awards in the bedroom department, but if I can learn to suck a dick, shouldn't he at least attempt to find my clitoris?

"It's not that hard to find," the bartender says, and I realize I said all of that out loud. Normally I'd be blushing, being this candid.

"Guys get off so easy, they just don't try."

The newcomer absorbs this. "The right guy does."

The bartender nods.

"In fact," the big guy continues, "the right guy makes sure the lady comes first, second, and third."

My mouth drops open.

"It's true," the bartender says with a twinkle in his baby blues.

"That's impossible," I breathe.

"You've never come multiple times?"

"I've never come with a guy before." With my first few partners, I faked it in case it hurt their feelings. With Jerry, I didn't even bother.

"What?" the bartender stares at me.

The big guy swivels on the stool and gets in my space, leaning over me, intent. “Is that true, baby? Never?”

“Never ever.” I hold his gaze for a moment. There’s something I’m forgetting. I wrinkle my forehead, trying to remember. “What’s your name?” I ask the big guy.

“Bear.”

“Bear.” I repeat. “Teddy Bear?”

“No, just Bear.”

“As in, he’s ‘big as a bear,” the bartender puts in.

“Well, that’s legit,” I say, leaning back to take Big Bear in. If I hugged him it’d be a challenge to get my arms around him.

This time the bartender doesn’t bother to hide his laugh. “Evie, where have you been all my life?” Did I tell him my name? Guess so. I cock my head to the side as he reaches over the bar and tucks a piece of hair behind my ear. His blond locks are long enough, I can do the same to him. So I do. He shakes his head, chuckling.

“Tomorrow night you drink free,” he winks at me.

“Oh, I don’t do this a lot,” I blurt. Is he flirting with me? I don’t quite know what to say. “I just had a bad day and needed a break.” I didn’t date Jerry long, but break ups are never easy. Or maybe I want to wash his final cruel words away.

Talking to this hot bartender will cure all my ills. He’s all smiles and charm, his blond hair glowing, a bright sun in a dark bar.

“Maybe you need to work out some tension.” He grins, and my insides curl. Dang, he *is* flirting. Normally I’d blush, make my excuses and hide, but no longer. I’ve sworn off men forever. I no longer care.

“What do you suggest?” I toy with my hair. Pretty and coy, that’s me.

"I can think of something," the bartender starts when Bear clears his throat. The big guy has been watching us closely.

"Not tonight," he says, fixing me with a somewhat stern look.

"Aww," I pout.

"Not tonight," the bartender confirms. "But later. Would you be up for a little game?"

"Sure." My voice sounds breathy. "I like games."

"Good." The bartender glances at Bear, who's frowning. "What?" he says to his customer. "She's perfect." I get a little thrill, and he turns back to me. "One of us will call you." One of us? What's up with that? Is this some sort of tag-team?

On TV, some ball player does a sport thing that's good for his team, and the men in the bar watching erupt in cheers. I clap my hands along with them, enjoying the sporty atmosphere. Normally I'd be home, licking my wounds and eating junk, wishing I could stick to a diet so I could land a decent guy, but my last conversation with Jerry made me so angry, I jerked my car into the sports bar's parking lot and stalked in.

"So, what's the game?" I ask as the place quiets down. "Like pool?"

"Do you like pool, sweetheart?" Bear asks. *Sweetheart.* How nice.

"I've never played. I have to warn you; I suck at most games."

"You won't suck at this. Or, you might say, the harder you suck, the better you'll be." The bartender winks at me.

Ohhhh. I nod and try to look worldly. "It's a sex game." I try to wink back at the bartender and blink instead.

"Tomorrow," the big guy says firmly, speaking more to

the bartender than to me. "We'll talk tomorrow when everyone has a clear head."

"Okie-dokie. I should go." I hop off the barstool and wait a moment for the room to stop spinning before fumbling for my wallet.

Big Bear's large hands come to my sides and steady me.

"I got it," he says and nods at the bartender, who nods back. "And I'm calling you a taxi."

"Oh, no need, I can Uber," I hiccup.

"A taxi," he rumbles and turns to the bartender. "Call Max." The blond nods and heads for the phone.

"Who's Max?" I ask. I wish I could remember the thing I'm supposed to remember.

"A taxi driver I trust. And when you're home, you need to drink more water before you go to bed."

I attempt to roll my eyes. "Yes, dad. You gonna come tuck me in?"

"Not this time."

Cue my blush, spreading over my chest, advancing up my neck.

I reach the door and turn, swaying on my feet. Bear looms over me. Beyond him, the bartender gives me a wave. I return it. Two hotties in one night. Shame I made a vow.

"Do you have someone who knows you're here?" Bear asks. "Someone you can call when you get home?"

"Uhhh... no."

"Give me your cell." His hand dwarfs my phone. He finishes programming his number in as the taxi drives up. "There. Text me when you get home." He walks me to the cab and opens my door. "Make sure she gets inside," he instructs Max.

"Sure thing, Bear." A pause, and I realize Bear is handing Max a few bills.

I roll down the window. Rain mists over my face, waking me up a little. The thing I'm supposed to remember nags from the back of my brain.

Bear finishes paying for my ride and leans over me.

"Remember to text," he orders. "I'll call you tomorrow."

"You will? Why?"

He cocks his head to the side. "To check on you."

"You don't have to do that."

"I want to."

My thoughts tug and shout at me, but I don't understand. "Uh... thanks."

"No problem, baby," he murmurs. "It's my pleasure."

"Mine too." Oops, a little too forward. I blink to disguise my lust-filled eyes. "Bye."

"Bye, baby."

The car glides off and I wave. I can't help the happy warmth that fills me, knowing Bear's waiting on the sidewalk to watch me go.

At 10:15 on a Tuesday, the mall parking lot is nearly empty. Which is good, because it means there aren't many witnesses to my pre-shopping panic attack.

This always happens. The shaking, the cold sweats. I sit in the car, wishing I could just leave. My hangover isn't helping. I don't know if the sick feeling in my stomach is from legit queasiness or dread.

My phone lights up with the Darth Vader theme from Star Wars.

"Perfect," I mutter and answer. "Hey, Auntie Jen."

"Evangeline," she trills, and I wince at the sound of my full name. "Have you got a dress?"

"Was just going shopping now."

"Wonderful!" I hold the phone away from my ear as she prattles at full volume and speed. "Remember, something in black. Black is perfect for you—it's slimming. Of course, you know that." She fake laughs. "I know the family expected you to be a bridesmaid but the floral pattern in cream... well you know. Patterns aren't very flattering on someone even a little overweight. And cameras add ten pounds."

"Yeah, Auntie Jen, I get it." I'm a fatty. Not the first time she's pointed this out.

"It's just too bad the diet I told you about didn't go well. Genevieve would've loved to have you in the wedding party."

My cousin Genevieve, the family darling. We were born on the same day but couldn't be more opposite. She's perfect. Beauty queen. Homecoming queen. Now she'll be the first of us to get married. Of course, all my other cousins are younger and boys, but it makes my failure all the more obvious.

It's not a competition, but it is.

"Don't worry, I'll find a dress. If anyone wonders why I'm wearing black to a wedding, I'll tell them floral prints make me look like a couch."

"Oh, Evangeline, you're so funny." Another fake laugh. Or maybe it's a real laugh. It sounds super fake. "Remember, black is your color. Bye now."

She hangs up and I get out of the car, slamming the door. How did my cousin get all the grace, poise, and beauty in our generation, plus a metabolism that could burn through a brick wall? It wouldn't be so bad if Auntie Jen didn't consider cellulite worse than a criminal record. It doesn't matter that I'm generally a decent person. As soon as I outgrew a size four, I was officially the family's black sheep.

At least black is slimming. Do black sheep look less fat than white ones? Are sheep even fat? Or do they just look that way because of their wool?

I stomp into the giant department store entrance, already wishing I could skip shopping and head straight to the frozen yogurt shop.

"Can I help you?" a saleswoman practically leaps on me.

"Just looking." I continue ripping through the hanging dresses and the lady retreats from my scowl. After a few minutes, I find two appropriate dresses—black—and ready myself for the dreaded dressing room. Mirrors are never my friend but dressing room mirrors are the worst. I swear they're all warped in a way that adds inches to my hips. They've never failed to leave me disappointed in myself. I end up vowing to go on a crazy diet, which leaves me wracked with hunger pains until I rip into a Häagen-Dazs while ugly crying. Which gives me more reason to hate myself.

And now I'm tearing up in a department store. Pathetic.

My phone rings again and I get a flash of relief at the generic ringtone. Talk about saved by the bell.

The name on the screen isn't familiar, but my neurons stir at the sight: Bear.

"Hello?"

"Hey, baby." Deep, rumbly voice, almost a purr. Oh yeah, the memory is coming back. Me, a bar, too much tequila, a guy with biceps big enough to be seen from space.

"Bear?" I croak.

"Yeah, baby. You okay?"

"Um... yes?"

"You didn't call."

Call? Was I supposed to—

Ooooh. He asked me to call him.

"Sorry, I... fell asleep. But I did drink water!" I crow. For some reason, I want him to know I obeyed.

"Good girl." His approval warms me all over.

"Thanks for... taking care of me."

"No problem."

"Can I just say... I'm never like that. I never get drunk like that in public."

"It's okay, baby. No harm in letting go once in a while."

"It was more that," I blurt. "I was having a bad day. My cousin is getting married, and I'm happy for her, but she's winning at life and I'm not." As I talk, I cover my face with my free hand. My blush is creeping up from my neck, spreading like a stain. I need to stop. But something about this guy just makes me want to share.

"Why do you say that?" No sign in the deep voice that I'm boring him with my patheticness.

"'Cause it's true. We're the same age. I've always been compared to her and I never come out looking good. For example," I take a deep breath, "She's a beauty queen and I'm... well, I'm me."

Silence.

Yeah, this is humiliating. But I've given up guys, and it's not like he's gonna date me, so it doesn't matter what I say. "And she's getting married and I just broke up with my boyfriend."

"He didn't sound like a keeper."

For a moment I'm confused. Did I tell him about my ex? Then last night's whole conversation comes flooding back and the crimson tide of my blush advances. I'm about to turn bright red in the middle of the department store.

And then it hits me: the thing I've been trying to remember. It shines in the daylight with horrific clarity: don't talk about not being able to orgasm with a man.

That's supposed to be a secret between me and my vibrator.

Damn tequila.

"Jerry was all right."

"He just didn't satisfy you." Bear's voice seems to get deeper.

"Um." I can't believe I overshared to two random guys at a bar. My cheeks are about to spontaneously combust. I duck behind a display lest the saleslady see. "No, he did not."

"Actually, that's why I'm calling. Sawyer and I have a proposition for you."

"Sawyer?"

"The bartender. We're friends from way back. We'd like to help you, and we think you can help us."

"Oh... 'kay."

"You free for lunch?"

"Um, today?" I glance around. My feet have already taken me towards the department store's exit. "I could be. I took off work this morning to run an errand." I take a step and the sliding doors open. Above, a bird wheels lazily in the clear blue sky. Freedom.

"Meet me at the bar at one. I'll buy."

"What, like a date?" I cringe. Of course, he didn't mean it like that. "I mean, I'm super busy today. And you know I've sworn off men forever." I try to joke, but it comes out serious.

Bear is silent. He's probably wishing he hadn't called. Gah! Why did I say the 'd' word?

"What's the proposition?" I ask as casually as I can. "I'm curious."

"I'd rather tell you in person." His voice is a low rumble.

"Oh? Is it something illegal?"

"No."

Dammit, nothing I'm saying is coming out right. "What is it? Just tell me." I detour from the exit and duck behind a shoe display.

"We want to help you orgasm."

Apparently, I died in the bar last night, because now I'm in heaven. Or hell. Either way, my head has exploded because it takes some time for me to choke out, "Excuse me?"

"Sawyer and I are competitive. We've always been, since we met. We try to see who's the best in everything."

Now I have no idea what he's talking about. But I can't hang up. The memory of his big body hovering protectively over mine is imprinted on me.

And my libido is wide awake and listening.

"We've argued for a long time who's better in bed. And this is our chance to find out. We talked about your situation last night and decided."

My thoughts are running in circles, but they focus for a second. "You talked about me?"

"Yeah, baby." Every time he says 'baby,' I melt a little bit more. "A woman like you should be satisfied in bed. You're perfect for our competition."

"What competition?"

"To see who's better in bed. We'll both sleep with you, get you off, and you'll be the judge."

I'm in the *Twilight Zone*. I'm on *Candid Camera*. In a second, someone's going to jump out and shout "'Surprise, sucka'!"

I gulp. "Why me?"

"You're a virgin."

"What? No, I'm not."

"You've never come with a man before," he points out.

There's no oxygen in the store. They really should do something about it. I'm surprised I haven't passed out.

"Maybe I can't," I say casually, as if I'm the sort of person who talks about her sex life with gorgeous strangers. Which, as of last night, I am.

The deep chuckle rumbles like thunder through the cellphone and stirs up things down below. I clutch a column to keep my knees from giving out. "I like a challenge."

"Well... okay."

A pause. "You agree?"

"I..." I have no idea what to say. On the one hand are two hot guys who want to compete to satisfy me in bed. On the other... what the hell is going on? "Are you sure you want me?"

The answer, when it comes, is gentle. "Yeah, baby."

I can't argue with that. What would I say? *I don't think I'm that attractive. I have cellulite. Are you sure you want me?*

"Just think about it. I'll call you later," he says, and hangs up, leaving me opening and closing my mouth like a fish in the middle of the men's section.

I HAVE no idea how I managed to exit the department store and drive to work, but at one pm I'm staring glassy-eyed at my desktop computer. Every once in a while I push the mouse so the screen saver doesn't appear. At 1:05 pm, my stomach rumbles. I could've been getting lunch with a gorgeous, considerate hunk of muscle and listening to his outrageous proposal. Maybe it's better that I didn't go. Looking deep into his brown eyes, there's no way I would be able to say no to anything.

"Evie!" My evil coworker, Ben, sails into my cubicle like

he owns it. "Did you get my email about the Billings account?"

"Not yet," I say. "Haven't checked email today. Very busy." *Busy freaking out.*

"Well, as soon as you do, I'll need your help organizing their expenses. They're expecting their final report tonight. You can stay late to do it."

Freakin' Ben. He always does this—comes by and spouts off about some account I've never heard of, and takes advantage of my confusion to dump more work on me.

"I wasn't going to stay late today."

"Why not?" he smirks as he eyes my admittedly dowdy work attire of a voluminous blouse, dumpy sweater. My skirt was rejected by the Amish as too conservative. "Got a date?"

"Maybe I do," I straighten. "Now if you'll excuse me—" I face my computer and click my mouse several times. Unfortunately, the first thing it lands on is my email spam folder, enlarging an email marketing a penis enhancement product. Gah! I click frantically, but instead of deleting it, I end up on the product website. GIVE HER MAXIMUM PLEASURE screams the flashing banner. A delighted cartoon dude's—ahem—member grows from a string bean to the size of a butternut squash. I mash the keyboard and the banners multiply, until a thousand cartoon men fill my screen.

"Well," Ben drawls. "I'll leave you to it."

As soon as he goes, I get rid of the freaking web pop ups and delete the email. My phone rings and I'm so flustered I answer it without checking.

"Evangeline!" my aunt sings. "So glad I got a hold of you. Listen, the florist we were going to use went out of business. Would you believe, last night their warehouse exploded. Rose petals rained down in the street. All those gladiolas! I don't like to gossip, but my friend Gwen thinks it was a front for the mob."

"Okay..." I keep clicking through my spam folder, waiting for her to get to the point.

"Anyway, we need to find a new florist. But your cousin's so busy—did you know her fiancé is taking her on a cruise next week? Isn't that sweet? He's just the best."

"He's a great guy," I agree, wondering what would happen if I just hung up. She'd probably show up at my work place and tell me all of this loudly, in person.

"Finishing up her work, shopping for new swimwear, she's too swamped. And you know how busy I am. So, we were thinking you could help us find a new florist. Coral rosebuds, not pink. There's a difference. And a forty percent discount. We won't accept anything less."

"Auntie Jen, I'm busy. I can't—"

"Of course, I already told your cousin that you'd be happy to help. She's so relieved. It's not like you have anything else to do after work. You don't have a man. Which reminds me, my workout class has a bring a friend free day next week. If you do a good job on the flowers—"

"Right. Fine," I say to get her off the phone. "Gotta go. My boss is coming by and I'm not supposed to take personal calls at work."

"But you're on your lunch break, right? You're not eating, I hope. You know what would be good for you? A brisk walk around the block. Your cousin—"

"Goodbye, Auntie Jen." I hang up and rub my head. I'll do the florist thing, just to keep her off my back. That way, when she invites me to go to her aerobics class, I can beg off and claim I am still looking for the right shade of coral rosebuds.

1:35 pm. I could've been eating hot wings and smiling at

Bear. Scratch that, I should never eat around guys. Don't want them wondering how many muffins are in my muffin top. Besides, I might spill sauce or crumbs on myself. The safest thing to eat: a few wilted lettuce leaves from a dressing-free salad. I agree with Auntie Jen on this one.

My phone rings and I cringe. Auntie Jen probably has another chore for me. Walking my cousin's dog while she's on the cruise. Baking the wedding cake from scratch. She'll make me wear a ball gag so I won't be tempted to lick the bowl. *"Safer this way, Evangeline—frosting is all fat and sugar! Goes straight to your hips."*

But when I check my phone, it's a number I don't recognize. I let it ring through and a minute later, my phone vibrates to notify me about a voicemail.

I snatch it up and listen.

"Hey, Evie," a smooth, familiar tenor. "It's Sawyer."

I nearly drop the phone. Sawyer called me. Sexy bartender Sawyer!

"—Bear told me he talked to you and... yeah. I just wanted to make sure you had my number. Call me."

Call me. I'm in the Twilight Zone. It's the end times. Earth must be about to be struck by a meteor. There's no way someone so hot and buff and tan would call me, drab little Evie of Johnson Accounting, round as I am tall, wearing Amish rejects.

My hands are shaking. I've got so many thrills running through me; my arms break out in goosebumps. My hair stands on end, like I've been electrocuted. *Call me.*

I can't call him. I've lost the ability to speak. But maybe I can text him.

I pull up his number and save it. Should I message him right away? No. I am very busy and important.

I ignore Sawyer's number as long as I can stand. I even

work on the stuff Ben sent over and email it back, which is dumb because he just responds by dumping another client case file on me, deadline tomorrow morning. At this rate, I'll be working until midnight.

Finally, at 2 pm, I send Sawyer a text.

Hey. The world's most scintillating opening. I bite my lip, willing him to text back.

2:08 pm, my phone blips.

Hey girl.

Oooh, classic. My insides are syrup.

I cover my face. I am texting a guy at work and blushing like a high school kid with a crush. That giddy flying feeling —my practical pumps no longer touch the ground.

A minute passes and I panic. Did I come on too strong? Was I not supposed to text him first? Is he sitting there judging me? Maybe he's at work. Is the bar open?

I click to the bar website.

"Ahem." my boss clears his throat behind me.

I tab over quickly to a spreadsheet before spinning my chair around to face him. "I was just um... looking into a potential new client. Owns a bar."

"I see." Mr. Johnson looks down his nose at me. "If you have time to solicit new clients, perhaps you can help Ben with a few of his accounts."

"Okay. Yes," I wilt in my chair and bend over my keyboard, all contrite. He walks away and I grab my phone again. I'm going to craft the most perfect text. Sawyer will be in awe. He will fall in love, propose marriage, and we'll have twin blond babies before my cousin's second anniversary.

At the very least, he'll text me back.

After ten minutes, I've got it.

What are you wearing? I text to Sawyer. I go back and

forth on emoji choices, finally settling for a winky face. I'm coy, I'm cute. I'm fucking hilarious.

Oh, who am I kidding? I'm pathetic. I'm going to be relegated to being my cousin's personal assistant with dog watching duties for the rest of my life. Always a bridesmaid, never a bride—except I'm never a bridesmaid, either. Bridesmaid would be a step up.

I slump over my desk.

My phone vibrates, and I pop up like the demon possessed girl in the Exorcist. I cringe when I see my *What are you wearing?* text. I could've done better.

Sawyer: *That's usually my line. Wink emoji.*

AHHHHHHHHHHHH!

I spin around in my chair. Ben walks by, frowning at me. It's almost three o'clock and I haven't gotten to my own client case files. I don't even care. I have left Earth and am sitting on cloud nine. Two hot guys, one day.

You're perfect for our competition. Bear growling on the phone. Sawyer's smooth tenor. *You're perfect for our competition.* Take that, Auntie Jen! I'm not too fat to attract male attention. *You're perfect.*

3:29 pm, my phone rings. Sawyer. I mime screaming before putting the phone to my ear. Deep breath, Evie. Be cool. Answer the phone.

"Hey." My voice is a breathy melody. Alto meets Marilyn Monroe. I hope. It's also possible I sound asthmatic.

"Hey girl." Sawyer could give Ryan Gosling sexy lessons. If he could bottle his voice into cologne and sell it, the scent would get a girl pregnant at twenty paces.

"Did he tell you?" There's a smile in Sawyer's voice. I clutch the phone tighter. The competition. Bear. Sawyer. Me.

"Yeah," I let out a shaky breath. "Is he for real?"

"Oh yeah," Sawyer laughs. "He's always for real. Truth is, we've been thinking about doing this for a long time. Just needed the right opportunity."

"And that's me?"

"That's right."

"Huh," I say, and he laughs.

"Come on. It'll be fun. You can't say you don't want to."

"Oh, I want to..." I trail off, imagining these two guys towering over me, taking my hand and leading me into a bedroom. Unreal, and yet my body sings to life. "I just don't know if it will be... wise."

"We'll make it worth your while." His voice vibrates through me.

"Do you do this a lot?"

"Nope. Like I said, we've been waiting for the right one to come along."

I weigh his words. The *right one* sounds nice, but maybe they were waiting for someone pathetic and desperate enough to say *yes* to something this crazy. That would explain why they picked me.

"I don't even know you guys."

"Get to know us," he coaxes. He has an answer for everything. "We can spend time together... not fucking."

"I don't date," I say automatically. Somehow this line has become my shield.

"We know," he soothes. "You've made that clear. Think of this as... exploring. For mutual benefit. C'mon, Evie," he adds when I hesitate. "Live a little."

"A little? What about living large?" As soon as I say it, I curse myself. I'm already large. Don't remind him.

"Sounds good to me. If you're with us, you better get used to large."

"Oh my," I warble, not even trying to be funny. Sawyer laughs.

"You are too cute."

Cute! I'm cute! "So I've heard." I twirl my hair on my finger, channeling suave and sophisticated. My finger snags on a knot. I tug but it's stuck.

"What're you doing tonight?"

"Brushing my hair." I yank my finger out and a chuck of my scalp comes with it. I bite back a yelp.

Sawyer chuckles. "Not washing it?"

"Oh, you know, I gotta save something for weekends." I rub my stinging scalp. "My life is so glamorous."

"Well, if you get your hair done early, come on by the bar. I'll be working seven to two."

"Uh, okay. I'll see what I can do. I've got a lot of hair." *I've got a lot of hair?* I pull the phone away and make a face. What the hell is wrong with me?

"You do that. Oh, and Evie," his voice drops an octave. "I'm not wearing anything."

AT FIVE THIRTY PM, I walk out of work like a zombie. After Sawyer's last words on the phone, I had a heart attack. I died. If I hadn't died from his sexy voice, I would've after imagining him at home, naked. Talking to *me.*

Zombie Evie gets herself home and changes into comfy clothes—stretchy leggings, oversized sweatshirt—and plays on her phone. I can't get the guys out of my head. I end up staring at my laptop, emptying my personal email inbox. Ninety percent of my life I spend staring at screens. Maybe it's about time I got out and did something. Or someone. Or two someones...

My phone rings and I almost drop it. I didn't realize I was holding it. It's Bear. Now I know I'm in the afterlife.

"Hello?"

"Hey baby," Bear rumbles. His voice is chocolate fudge ice cream covered in chocolate sauce. I've gained five pounds just listening to it.

"Hey." I curl up on the couch, hoping he'll keep talking. I sure as hell don't know what to say.

"Sawyer said he called you."

"Yep. He did. Sawyer called me. We talked." I close my eyes. Got to shut up.

"And? What do you think?"

"Did my cousin pay you off?" I blurt. "This is a setup, right?" A little elaborate for a joke, but I wouldn't put it past Genevieve.

Silence.

"I mean," I try to infuse a little humor into my accusation. "It just seems a little far-fetched. Hi, we both want to sleep with you. Like, haha."

More silence. I squeeze the shit out of my phone.

"I mean, I just don't see... I don't know... you both want to sleep with me..."

"Is it so hard to believe we'd want to sleep with you?"

"Um, yeah."

"Why?" He sounds thoughtful. I squirm on the couch.

"I don't know. Maybe because... you could get any girl you want?"

"Is that so?" He sounds amused. Thank God. "Right now the girl we want is you."

"Oh. Right," I say. Lame. "Well, I'm flattered—"

"Dinner, tomorrow night."

"Wh-what?"

"We jumped the gun, I get that. You need to know we're

serious. To know that, you need to know us. We'll start slow. You, me, dinner. We can head to the bar after and have drinks with Sawyer."

"Um," I squeak. My heart is fluttering. He just takes charge.

"Tex's Steakhouse. Route 5. Seven pm. I'll meet you there. Unless," he pauses. "Unless you'll let me pick you up."

"Meeting there is fine," I say, and shake my head. I just agreed to have dinner. "Uh, does this place have salads?"

"Babe," he's back to amused.

"I, uh, I'm not sure about this..."

"Dinner, seven pm. I'll be a perfect gentleman. Wear a dress." He says goodbye in that deep and decadent voice of his, calls me baby one more time and hangs up.

"I'm having dinner with a guy tomorrow night," I say out loud, to test it. "He'll meet me there. He'll be a perfect gentleman." Did this just happen? "It did," I tell myself. "It just happened."

My phone vibrates. *You do dinner with him; you get drinks with me. 5pm. Tell him to pick you up at the bar.* Sawyer, one upping Bear. Of course. It's a competition. That's all this is.

I don't get off until 530. I text.

Six, then. He shoots back. He and Bear both have record levels of bossy.

I think I like bossy.

Fine. Do I really have to wear a dress? Bear says so.

Wear a skirt, Sawyer orders. *Don't let him tell you what to do.*

If I wear a skirt, I'm doing what YOU told me to do. I reply.

Exactly.

I laugh out loud. *Maybe I'll just wear jeans.*

Tight jeans. He counters.

My face falls. All my jeans are tight. I have a huge ass.

I drop my phone and get off the couch. My stomach is grumbling, but I should skip dinner.

My phone buzzes while I'm perusing my fridge contents. I grab a bag of baby carrots and amble back to the couch.

Evie?

I'm here. Just getting dinner. About to start brushing my hair. I type back, feeling a bit morose all of a sudden.

K. Wouldn't want to distract you from the hair brushing.

Yeah, it takes concentration. I crunch my carrots and fight off depression.

Wear whatever you want tomorrow. We don't care, as long as you come.

According to Bear, I'll be coming a lot.

You bet your sweet ass. He adds a smiling demon emoji that makes me giggle.

I polish off the baby carrots, feeling better.

After that, Sawyer's texts are less frequent. Makes sense, he's working. I give in and eat a fast food chicken sandwich, leftover from last night. It's crunchy and has my yearly dose of sodium. Oh well. I need calories to keep up with these guys. How many calories do you burn during a ménage à trois?

Stop it, Evie. I toss the chicken sandwich wrapper, dust off my hands and grab my computer. Time for some good old-fashioned social media stalking.

I open Facebook. Should I make a fake profile? Would they friend me? I consider fake names. *Sabrina Townsend.* She sounds nice. Maybe not flirty enough. *Cherry Licksalot.* That's better.

Or maybe I just friend them as little ol' me. See if they accept. I friend request them both and slam down my laptop.

I spend the next five hours pacing back and forth,

avoiding checking my computer. At least, it feels like five hours. Maybe more like five minutes before I throw my computer open. I have no self-control.

I scroll back to Facebook, holding my breath.

They accept! We are officially friends! I don't know if it warrants a happy dance, but I do a butt wriggle. I crack my knuckles and start scrolling.

Bear likes cars, the more muscle-y the better, and Sawyer likes the beach. And they take almost no selfies. There's nothing on their walls beyond photos they're tagged in. Parties with friends or family barbecues. Pictures of Bear at the gym, with muscles that make my mouth water. Pictures of Sawyer surfing probably snapped by a glamorous bikini babe who was also his girlfriend. Sawyer has posted a few black and white pictures of the surf and sand with Ansel Adams-like qualities.

I resist the urge to wallpaper my computer with Bear & Sawyer shirtless montages. I can't get involved with these guys until I know what they're up to. They don't think anything is wrong with me... so something must be wrong with them. Right?

That's messed up. They could just really like you.

Or they're serial killers.

I need more.

I Google their names and get pictures of Bear at a car show, posing with a model, and Sawyer at a beach party with what looks like the top three contestants in a wet t-shirt contest. It's obvious they can get any girl they want, any time. So why do they want me?

I need to know these guys. I need to know what game they're playing. I need a professional level stalker, and I know just who to call.

"Hey, bitch," Mina sings cheerfully. "What's happening?"

"Do you have to call me that?"

"You know how I like to swear. It's a term of endearment."

"Fine." I shake my head. "I need you to look into someone. Two someones."

"Oh?" Mina drawls, but I can tell she's super interested.

I give her Bear and Sawyer's full names.

"What?" Her voice gets clearer, and the sound of typing rushes like a waterfall in the background. Even in high school, Mina was a super nerd—the kind who learns to program before she can drive and tries to hack NASA's firewall for fun. "They were in school with my older brothers. What's going on with them?"

My cheeks color just saying it. "They kinda want to... play with me."

"What!" Mina shrieks. "Both of them? Damn, I leave town and you have all the fun." The sound of typing intensifies.

I look around my empty apartment, bare of life except for the cactus I haven't managed to kill yet. His name is Spiny.

It's nine at night, I had not one but two invitations to go out and flirt with not one but two insanely hot guys, and I am hiding. I am the human equivalent of a hermit crab. *Yeah, fun.* "Just... see what you can dig up on them."

"On it. I'll get you a report. Credit report, background check, arrest record, evidence of crazy exes on social media—you will know all."

I suck in a breath. "Thanks."

"No problem, bitch. You're my bestie. Mina out." The line goes dead and I rub my forehead. This is exhausting. How did people research their hookups in the olden days, before the internet? Climb a tree and look through binoculars?

At least I have a plan. I'll go out tomorrow night, get more details about this competition. Tell the guys I need to think about it. Mina will report back that these guys do this all the time, sucker women in, and leave them crying at the altar. Then I can gracefully bow out and move on.

I'll try not to be too disappointed.

After a shower and grooming session—it does take me awhile to take care of my hair—I'm curled up in bed and dozing. I never went out to the bar. Does that make a coward? Probably. If I were the happy glamor girl these guys think I am, I'd be out partying, not hiding in my apartment, the four white walls that mark the boundaries of my sad little life. But I can't change for a guy. Not even if I kinda want to.

My phone buzzes.

Sorry you didn't make it out. Sawyer. I send him a sleepy face emoji. *Zzzzzz.*

Remember, tomorrow. 6pm. Tight jeans.

Bear said 7 at the restaurant.

I already told him the new plans. Bear can have you later. I get you first.

Omigod. I cover my face with my hands. With everything going on, I haven't had time to shop for a vibrator. But dang, if I had it, I'd use it tonight.

I'm about to put my phone away and pass out when my phone vibrates insistently. I expect another text from Sawyer, but this is a voicemail from Bear. I must have missed his call when I was in the shower.

"Hey, Evie." His deep voice makes my stomach flip flop. "Sawyer told me about the change of plans. I'll see you at Ballers. And... I know I hit you with a lot today. Didn't mean to freak you out." A pause. He's weighing his words. Such a nice guy. "We don't have to move forward if you don't want to. Obviously. But think about it. We really want you." Another pause. I listen like my life depends on it.

"Night, baby."

We really want you. Error. Does not compute. The confession didn't sound like a man who wanted another notch in his bedpost. It sounded like a man speaking from his heart, to a woman he cared about. Gentle.

He isn't a player. Nothing signaled that to me. But they did propose a game.

The question is, when the game is over, could I fit myself back into the confines of my old life?

I sink back into my pillows, gnawing on my lip. *We really want you.* New reality. Mind blown. Is my life about to change?

No, it already has.

CHAPTER 2

The next morning, I sit at my desk silently freaking out. Tonight is dinner with Bear, and drinks with Sawyer. How did I go from 'not dating' to meeting with two men? I can't even remember agreeing. I've packed makeup and a change of clothes, so I won't be late.

"Evie, boss said you can help me with this," Ben rolls by, slapping a client file down on my desk and walks off, cell phone to ear. I bare my teeth at his back and get to work. I skip lunch, but after three missed calls from my aunt reminding me about my florist finding duties, I slip out to hand deliver a file to a client who likes a personal touch. On the way, I stop at a florist and end up comparing shades of pink.

After a while they all blur together. When I finally find the right rosebuds, the florist starts brandishing baby's breath. Why the hell can't my cousin pick out her own flowers?

On a whim, I text Sawyer.

I'm making a decision and I need advice.

The reply comes as I'm reviewing costs with the florist. *Yes, to the push up bra, no to the panties.*

My blush rolls up the slope of my breasts. I excuse myself from flower picking and duck down an aisle of funeral displays. *What?*

I assumed you wanted to know what to wear tonight?

No! Real quick: white or purple?

Purple, Sawyer answers. *What's this for? A sex toy?*

I snicker. *Maybe.*

Tease.

I exit the florist and float down the sidewalk. *Be good and I'll let you play with it later.* I've never let myself text such outrageous things, but Sawyer brings out the best in me. Or is it the worst?

That's my line.

When I walk into the office, my smile is so wide, Ben does a double take. "Where were you?" he asks.

"Delivering the Nguyen file to the law firm. Mrs. Nguyen says hi."

His eyes narrow, gears grinding as he wonders what the lawyers did to put a smile on my face.

I check my phone when I'm safe in my cube.

Sawyer's texted, *See you tonight.*

Yep, this is happening. I can't suppress my big dopey grin. *You know, I never actually agreed to tonight.*

But you're coming, right?

Maybe. Depends on the state of my hair.

How many times do you need to brush it?

As many as it takes to get it untangled.

Little elliptical dots dance as he thinks of a reply. I hold my phone under my desk, my knee jiggling. I'm a text-junkie.

Finally, his text comes through. *Can I help?*

I laugh out loud. This is gonna be so fun.

I WALK into Sawyer's place of work at six pm sharp. *A red head, a surfer, and a muscle man walk into a bar.* I try to think of a joke, but all I come up with is a threesome.

Sawyer's at the bar, polishing glasses, his blond head a flash of sunlight in the dim bar. I like the low lights in this place. I feel more comfortable in the dark. Easier to hide my flaws.

How sad. How much of my life is ordered around my body insecurity? I didn't realize how much it controlled me. Maybe that's why I hide in my apartment when two hot guys take an interest.

I cross the room. I'm wearing a stretchy black skirt that hugs my hips and a V-neck top that flatters my boobs. No Amish rejects today. I almost feel good. I can cozy up to the bar, cleavage on display, and flirt with Sawyer. I'll stick to water, so I don't make a fool of myself. I can't keep a lid on my mouth when I'm not tipsy, and we've already established that I have no filter around these guys. Who knows what would come out if I drink again?

I get halfway to the bar and halt.

There's a thin blonde planted on a bar stool. Her legs are thin and eight miles long, stacked on stilettos. Toothpicks teetering on toothpicks. She crosses and uncrosses her legs, posing. She could be a model. She leans over the bar, laughing at something Sawyer says, white teeth flashing.

I can't sit next to her. I'll look like the 'before' in the 'before and after' extreme skinny diet pictures. I can't compete.

Is it too late to run for the door?

Sawyer turns. His eyes snag on me. Too late to run. I give a little wave.

His face lights up when he sees me. "There she is." I roll forward, Sawyer's greeting bolstering me.

The babe at the bar sits back, eyes darting between me and Sawyer, checking for clues to our relationship.

"All right, let's see it," Sawyer says as I get closer.

"You want to see it?" I raise my brows, putting a hand to my hair.

He spreads his hand, getting into the joke. "You're gonna make me wait?"

I pretend sigh and tug out my fancy comb, letting my hair wash over my shoulders in shining auburn waves. Flaws aside, I have damn good hair.

"Very nice," Sawyer nods, taking on the air of a connoisseur. I flip my hair, letting him peruse the shining skein. "Very clean."

I grin. The blonde gives me a weird look but basking in the light of Sawyer's smile I can ignore her. *That's right, we have an inside joke.* I slide onto the barstool and try not to compare the size of my ass to Miss Perky Tits beside me.

"Whatcha drinking?"

"Um..." I should say water. I was going to order an appetizer so I can drink but there's no way I can eat in front of Miss Skinny. "Surprise me."

With a wink, he grabs bottles and mixes something up that tastes mostly of fruit juice.

"Mmm, yummy. What is this?"

"Sex on the beach." The twinkle in his eye could make a girl pregnant. My ovaries tingle.

Yowza. "I like."

"There's more where that came from." He gives me another wink and I nearly fall off the stool.

Now the blonde is really studying me. Scanning me up and down, cataloguing all my flaws and labelling me as "non-competition." I'm used to such scans. Auntie Jen does it all the time and taught me and my cousin to do them starting at age thirteen. My cousin doesn't do them so much anymore because she's likely to be the thinnest, prettiest and sweetest girl in the room. I do one of my own on the blonde and come up with a depressing ten outta ten. My boobs and hair barely get me to a five.

Blondie smirks like she knows this.

"Be right back," Sawyer swaggers to the back. Both of us swivel on our stools to watch his fine backside.

Blondie turns to me. "Sawyer is, like, so hot."

"Mhmm," I agree vigorously, even though he is not '*like*' so hot, he '*is*' so hot.

"Are you, like, with him?"

"Um…" Oh no, I'm gonna blush. The flush starts at my chest and rolls upward, a telling red tide. "We're just working on something together."

The blonde's eyebrows knit together. She can't quite figure it out, me and him. *You and me both, sister.*

I sip my drink and watch the blonde fight to categorize me as "not a threat." If she wants him, she can have at him. A hot guy like Sawyer should pay attention to a ten outta ten over me. If he ignored me and flirted with her, I'd be disappointed but fine. All would be right with the world.

"Evie." A rumble at my back makes me turn.

Warmth rolls up my back, Bear's voice like a blanket settling over my shoulders.

Blondie's eyes are round as dinner plates. We both crane our necks to look up at the mountain that is Bear. He bends and kisses my cheek.

Oh my. There go my panties.

"Hey," I hug him and grab my drink like a shield, sipping it to hide my expression.

"What you drinking?"

"Sex on the beach."

His gaze heats. I sway on the stool.

"You hungry?"

"Yes," I say before I can rethink it. I'm supposed to pretend I'm only a wee bit peckish and stick to a salad.

My stomach chooses this moment to growl. "I didn't eat lunch," I admit.

A disapproving look. "Baby, you gotta eat."

My stomach agrees.

"Are you okay to drink on an empty stomach?"

Probably not. "Umm..."

"I'll order us some wings. Any allergies?"

I shake my head. Bear heads off to confer with Sawyer, who has re-emerged from the back. I run a finger around the rim of my glass. I didn't think Bear could get any sexier, but him insisting on feeding me is my new favorite thing ever.

The blonde leans in quickly. "Are you with both of them?" Her eyebrows shoot so far up her forehead they almost disappear into her hair.

"Uh..." my blush marches across my face, unfurling a red flag of shame. "It's sorta a group project."

Bear returns with a beer and settles a hand on my back. We make small talk while Sawyer serves up hot wings and gives me a glass of water. My resolve not to eat in front of the guys dissolves at the sight of buffalo sauce. Bear seems to like feeding me as much as I enjoy it. At least, he watches me with a crinkle around his eyes, nursing his beer, looking pleased. I forget myself and fill my belly. Bear 1, Diet 0. Poor Blondie fidgets, trying to catch Sawyer's eye, but finally gives up and heads to a table, head bowed. She's not used to being ignored.

I'm not used to attention, but I'll take it. Having two guys interested in me must have sprinkled some sort of alluring magic dust over me, because the minute Bear and Sawyer are distracted by a sports thing on the big TV, another guy sidles up to the bar and offers to buy me a drink.

"I'm good," I say, hoping he won't insist. I don't have to say anything more, because Bear steps close. His arm slides around my shoulders, an obvious signal. Guy code: back off, this one's mine. In case the man can't read guy code, Bear says, "This one's taken."

My insides spasm happily. I try to hide it.

"If you're interested, she's single," I point to the blonde at the table, looking lost. The guy's eyes light at her ten outta ten good looks and he heads off.

I swivel to face Bear. His arm loosens but doesn't go away. "Taken, huh?"

He dips his head close. "You thought any more about our offer?"

It's only all I can think about. "Maybe."

"You gonna pick up other guys before giving us our answer?"

"No. You two are about all I can handle." I sound as flippant as if having two guys interested in me is something that happens every week, as mundane as laundry. "I'm just wondering... if I say yes to judging the competition, how is that going to work?"

Sawyer joins us. "I figure we take turns. One of us goes first, then the other. And we repeat a few times."

"In one night?" I squeak.

"I was thinking we take different nights, over the course

of a few weeks." Sawyer's eyes twinkle. "Unless you wanted to get it over with in one night—"

"That's all right," I say quickly. "I'd like to be able to walk afterwards."

Bear chuckles.

"A few weeks?" This is more involved than I thought.

"At least," Bear says. "We each get different nights, spread over a month. Give you time to recover."

I laugh weakly, but he seems dead serious. "A month seems really spread out."

"You won't be bored," Sawyer promises. "Foreplay is half the fun."

Foreplay? And I thought this was going to be *wham, bam, thank you ma'am,* times two. "Won't you guys be bored?" Alternate nights mean they'll be waiting their turns.

They exchange cryptic glances.

"Oh no, Evie," Sawyer says. "I think we'll be plenty entertained." He heads to get drinks for a crowd of workmen who just walked in. Bear hovers over my shoulder.

"Ready to go?"

The plate of wings is now a pile of bones. Oops. I'm not supposed to eat on dates. One of Auntie Jen's rules. I should protest about dinner and bow out so I'm not tempted to demolish a whole cow in front of him, forever losing the chance to convince him I'm as thin and poised as Blondie. But he puts a large hand on my back, the subtle scent of his cologne washing over me, and I'm helpless to resist.

I hop off the stool and his hand swallows mine.

"Say goodnight to Sawyer," Bear instructs.

"Goodnight, Sawyer."

"Be good," Sawyer calls back, winking at me, but pointing a more serious finger at Bear.

Dinner at Tex's turns out to be easier than I thought. My menu has no prices on it.

"You eat meat?" Bear asks before I can request a new menu.

I hesitate. Is that a double-entendre?

"Steak," he clarifies.

"Yes, definitely." Auntie Jen's voice screeches in my head and I add, "But I'm not really hungry."

"Hmmm," Bear looks skeptical.

The waiter comes and Bear orders for us both. I have a mini mental freak out over whether I can eat steak or not in front of a man and decide to take two bites before declaring myself stuffed. No touching the bread or mashed potatoes. Then Bear turns to me, asks about my work, and before I know it, I'm chatting about clients and tax deadlines and my desire to run my own firm. He listens with serious intent, like I'm the only person in the world.

Next time I look down, my plate is empty of all but crumbs. Oops. I'm sated with more than just food, drunk on Bear's attention. He even listens to me complain at length about having to go dress shopping.

"I mean, black is my color, but who wears black to a wedding? I'll look like the Grim Reaper."

"Who says black is your color?"

"Oh, my aunt."

"She blind?"

I sputter a laugh. "No. But she sees things a certain way. She has high standards, and I am not up to them."

"Hmm." His grunt makes me think he has a not very high opinion of my aunt.

Having fun? Sawyer texts.

Oh yes. This strip club has great food, I joke. *And I can dance off the calories.*

Take pictures! He sends back with about a million exclamation points. I smirk as I put my phone away.

"Having a good time?" Bear asks.

"Yeah." He and Sawyer are so in sync it's scary. Which reminds me of something I wanted to ask...

"Have you and Sawyer ever... you know," I lower my voice, "shared a woman before?"

"You gonna say yes to the competition?"

"Maybe." I toy with my fork. It's tempting, so help me.

Bear stretches an arm along the back of the booth, behind me but not touching. "What can we do to make you feel comfortable?"

"You're already doing a lot. And you never answered my question. Have you shared before?"

"A few times. Why? Do you want us to share you?"

I drop the fork with a clatter. My blush answers for me.

"We want you a few times alone," Bear muses. "But we can do a night all together. If you really want."

"I haven't said yes yet," I point out with as much dignity as I can muster while my blush marches across my face, taking no prisoners.

"Mmm," he murmurs, a finger lightly tracing my shoulder. "What are you doing Sunday night?"

"Nothing," I narrow my eyes.

"You want to meet up?"

"Like a date? I don't—"

"It's not a date. You gotta get comfortable with us." His big hand strokes my shoulder. It's nice. "Think of it as pregame. The carnival's in town."

"That sounds fun." And pregame makes it part of the competition.

"I'll pick you up at seven."

"If it's not a date, then I should just meet you there.

Although I would like to ride in one of your rumble cars sometime."

"Rumble cars?"

"The muscle cars you have all over your feed."

"All over my feed, huh?"

Uh oh, busted.

"You checking me out, baby?"

"I had to be certain you weren't serial killers," I tell him seriously.

Bear throws his head back with a body-shaking laugh, complete with flashing white teeth. Happiness curls through me.

"And you'd figure that out from my Facebook?"

"Well, you know. Women have built-in bastard radar."

Another chuckle. "Did I make the cut?"

"Yes. You and Sawyer. Will you both be at the carnival?"

His face goes blank. "You want us both there?"

"Uh, yeah, if I'm going to get to know you both. That's the point of this, right?" *Cause it's not a date.*

"Meet me at the carnival. It'll be you and me." His hand slides up my back and I fight the urge to arch like a cat. I'm already used to him touching me. "Sawyer can get you another time."

Is it wrong to love them fighting over me? This competition would be hella good for my self-esteem. Too bad I'm going to say no.

"The carnival," I agree, because even if I should break this off now, it's easier to resist chocolate cheesecake than say no to Bear.

CHAPTER 3

PREGAME

My fingers plucked the edge of my shorts as I wait by the carnival entrance. I don't often wear shorts, or a tank top this skimpy, but today is hot and I don't want to end up a sweaty mess. Amish wear is out. Besides, these shorts are loose enough that I feel comfortable in them. They won't ride up or stick to my legs. I usually don't wear them out of the house in case my aunt sees me and lectures me about showing cellulite.

The crowd parts and Bear emerges. The sun streams around his wide shoulders, the soft beams caressing his profile. If I listen hard, I can hear the faint chorus from a heavenly angel choir. Mr. Perfect.

He grins when he spots me, and I wave like a dork. Grin stretching under his mirrored shades, he ambles my way and looms over me. For a moment I'm afraid he'll kiss me in public and I'll melt into a puddle of goo, but he just puts his hand at my back. Again, with the touching. I could get used to this.

No, no, no. I will not get used to this. This is not a date. This is a pregame. Whatever that is. What does pregame entail? First through second base? When the competition starts, we will be jumping straight to third base. Homerun, right away. But now we have this pregame thingy. Does that mean we'll start at first base? What is first base anyway? From what I remember from school, it's kissing. Second base would be touching—on the naughty bits. In high school I called it groping, but Bear and Sawyer will have more finesse.

So, third base is sex. But what about shortstop? Is that oral? And if there are only three bases, how do we classify a ménage à trois? Is that a double header?

I suck at sports. And sports metaphors.

"Whatcha thinking about?" Bear asks me while we wander through the crowds. He bought food and beer and once again I forget my solid vow to never eat in front of a man. Another thing to think about.

"Uh, nothing."

"You've been frowning for the past five minutes."

So much for poker face. "I'm a little worried about all this," I say as offhandedly as I can.

Bear guides me to the side of the walkway and sets me to face him. "What if you didn't have to worry?" He tucks a strand of hair behind my ear. "What if you could just relax and let us do all the work?"

"Lie back and think of England?"

"I'd prefer you to think of me."

Shiver. "I could do that." I'm not sure if I can completely stop my brain, but Bear seems confident in what he's doing.

"You don't have to worry," he tells me, and the tension eases out of me as if I've been waiting all my life to hear someone say that. "Just let go and let me lead. Can you trust me?"

I open my mouth but before I can answer, I catch a glimpse of a familiar face.

"Oh no." My cousin and her perfect fiancé stroll up the walkway, flashing their thousand watt smiles, model ready. The carnival could take pictures of them and use them in advertising. *Happy couple having a fun time.*

I grab Bear's arm. "We gotta hide." I tug him into a random exhibit. He follows willingly, which is what allows me to pull him behind me in the first place. We emerge from a dark anteroom into a narrow hallway, where our distorted images bloat in all directions. Funhouse mirrors. Great. Because I don't fear my reflection enough.

"Why are we hiding?" Bear sounds amused.

"That was my cousin. I didn't want her to see us." I realize how insulting this sounds. "Not that I'm embarrassed to be seen with you. It's more that I'm embarrassed for you to be seen with me." We round a corner and I avoid looking at the reflection. "It'll get back to my aunt. She meddles. Besides, I'm not supposed to wear shorts..." I trail off, ducking down random corridors, trying to find my way out of this maze. "Aha!" I throw open a door painted black to match the walls, but it's a closet.

"Evie," Bear catches my arm. I risk a glance at the mirror's and focus on his reflection. His face is carefully blank. "Slow down. Why aren't you supposed to wear shorts?"

Crap. Shouldn't have said anything. "My aunt thinks my legs are too short for them to look good. I'm supposed to cover up."

A rumble that sounds like a growl. "What does she want you to wear?"

"I don't know. She's never satisfied. Maybe a burka? If it will get me off the hook to go wedding dress shopping, I'll seriously considered it. A burka, I mean." Gah, I'm rambling. "I think that's the way out." I start for the perceived exit but with a half growl, Bear pulls me back.

"Evie—"

"Can we just go? This place is freaking me out." Truth is, it's getting hard to avoid looking at the mirrors. I don't need to see myself in a fat mirror. I look fat enough in a regular one.

Without another word, Bear heads to the left, drawing me in his wake. We reach the exit and I heave a sigh. I peek out into the walkway. "They're gone."

It hits me as we enter the alley. Bear just got a front row seat to my particular brand of crazy.

I duck my head so my hair falls over my face. "Maybe we should just go."

"Evie—"

"I'm nuts." I shake my head, unable to meet his eyes. "That was psycho. I didn't mean for you to see that."

"Hey," he says, hands on my shoulders. "You're not ready for your family to see us. I get that. I got this."

"Okay," I mouth, still not looking at him.

"You didn't answer my question. Will you trust me?"

I bite my lip and nod.

"Out loud, Evie."

"I trust you."

"Thank you." He gives me a squeeze. "If we see your cousin, we can duck out. Unless you're tired...?"

"No." Now that my freak out is passed, I don't want to go home. "I want to stay. With you."

A detour to a stall and he buys a ball cap, settling it gently on my head.

"A disguise?" I joke.

"A memento."

Warm tendrils curl through my body. *No, no,* I scold. *No feelings. Feelings bad.*

It's not until we're sitting on a Ferris wheel, easing our way into the sky that I accept the happy feelings are here to stay. Bear keeps a hand on my back, stroking my hair. It's the most intimate I've felt with a man, and we have all our clothes on.

Our seats swing gently as we rise above the carnival. Night has fallen and the wind has a chill. I shiver a little and he tucks me into his side.

"Cold, baby?"

"I'm good." I study his features. His body is pure power, muscles hewn from rock. His face isn't handsome in the classical sense, but the dark eyes, strong nose, and blunt chin add to the image of masculine power. His jawline is so strong you could break a fist on it. Pick him up and set him down in another time, he'd be a warrior, a gladiator, a mountain of muscle who can hold off an army.

And somehow, with me, his voice and touch are so gentle. "Whatcha thinking?"

He followed me through the fun house and didn't freak out at my freak out. I might as well share.

"You asked me what I was thinking earlier. I said I was worried, but I also was thinking—during this pregame, what are the rules? Is there touching? Or more than touching? Like, first base? Although I'm not sure what first base is anymore. I figure third base is... *you know.*" I mouth the word 'sex' like it's a big secret. "But I forget which base is oral. And what about shortstop?"

I'm babbling but the corner of his mouth and eyes are crinkled in what I hope is amusement.

"The bases worked in high school, but now I think we need more stages. Maybe we could use a different sport for scoring." I think for a bit. "Like... tennis. First stage is love." My eyes widen when I realize what I've said. "Not actual love! That's just where you start. In tennis, I mean. 'Love' in tennis means 'nothing', though I don't understand why they use the word 'love' at all—"

Bear slants his head and brushes his lips against mine. My own lips part and his taste slices through me: heat and beer and a yummy flavor that's all Bear. His hand comes up and cups my cheek as his lips drink from mine, slow sips at first, then longer pulls, claiming more of me. His tongue slips into my mouth and electricity zings my nipples.

He pulls back and I feel slightly tipsy.

"First base," he says firmly.

Love. One kiss. Game, set, and match.

I am so screwed.

I WAKE the next day with the memory of Bear's kiss tingling on my lips. Overnight, the happy tendrils have grown from my heart, spread down my limbs and blossomed into coral-colored rosebuds.

So much for containing my feelings.

Then I remember my freak out. God, did I really say all that?

I half expect them to text me today, canceling everything. I don't know if I'd be disappointed or relieved.

Disappointed, definitely. But it'd probably be better to shut things down now, before I get really entangled. Right?

I settle in at my desk and tell myself sternly to focus. Ben has already left a bunch of his half-finished work on my desk. I don't have time for distractions. No logging into social media. No internet stalking allowed.

Until I get an email from Mina. It's one sentence: *Thunderbirds are go!*

I grab my phone. Eleven am is late enough to take lunch, right? I duck out to my car and call her.

"You're sure?" I say before she can greet me. "No shady stuff? At all?"

"Nothing. Bear owns a business—two businesses, actually. Mechanic plus body shop. They do well enough that he paid his brother back the initial investment, plus profit. Did you know Bear isn't his real name?"

"No... well, I figured it was a nickname."

"Yep. Anyway! Sawyer's a bit of a drifter, but he's a decent guy. Does photography on the side."

I'm not sure if I'm disappointed or exhilarated. "Did you look everywhere? Even social media?"

"Yep, and let me tell you, it was sooo hard, scrolling through all those pictures of Sawyer surfing. And Bear must work out all the time because... damn."

My stomach flips. I see shirtless montages in my future. I'm not as terrified as I should be.

Mina reads into my silence. "Why? Did you want me to find something?"

"No. No, it's okay. Thanks, Mina."

"You said they're interested in you?"

"No, it's more... it's more of a bet they have. I'm involved." I cover my face with my hand, feeling the blush creeping up. Good thing Mina can't see me.

"You gotta tell me about it. Most girls would give

anything to get involved with those two. Even in high school, those guys could get laid anytime they wanted."

"Yeah." Which is why it makes zero sense why they'd want to sleep with me. I can't forget that. "Thanks, Mina."

"You can pay me back by telling me everything, when I'm home for Thanksgiving."

"Sounds good." Whatever I have with Bear and Sawyer will be over by then. I'll have had my fun—or not—and this will be a memory. "I promise to tell you everything."

"I'll hold you to it." Mina says, and adds, "They're shit hot, girl. And so are you. Go get 'em."

I sit in the car for a million years, my hand fossilized around the cellphone. I have a decision to make. I'm in an Indiana Jones movie, on a scrap of rock between two chasms. On one side yawns the rest of my life, boring, spinster apartment, nights in. Eventually I will give into the urge and adopt loads of cats. Or at least get another cactus to keep Spiny company.

On the other are Bear and Sawyer. Prime grade beef steak. Tanned eight pack abs. Hard dicks. Soulful eyes. Headed my direction, in slow motion, the start of my own personal porno. They wanna be players? They want a competition? I'll give them the game of their life. They can fight over the trophy and give me orgasms.

Either way, I'll win.

I dial Bear. It rings and rings. *Come on, come on.* It runs straight to voicemail with a beep.

"Hey, it's Evie," I blurt before I lose my nerve. "I'm in."

"Baby." Bear rumbles into the phone. His deep voice contains a smile. My insides curl into pretty pink bows. Coral pink.

"Hey,"

I realize I'm twirling a strand of hair around my finger like the caricature of a mooning woman and yank my hand away.

"Nervous?"

"Maybe. I've never done this before."

"We'll go easy on you."

"Maybe I prefer hard." I cover my face as my blush marches up from my breasts to my neck, headed for my face. I've got to get the blushes under control, or every time I quip, I'll end up with a tomato face.

Bear chuckles, his laugh so deep and delicious I can taste it. Forget beef steak, he is chocolate lava cake. So bad for me, yet so damn good. "Don't worry, baby. You'll get both."

Squuuuueeeeeee.

"Come to lunch with me."

"I can't. Work. I already took my lunch break."

"Did you eat?"

No, I sat in my car after talking to Mina and hyperventilated. Then I left you a message. "Define 'eat'?"

"Evie." A tinge of disapproval in his voice, but not sharp and cutting like my aunt's. He cares. "You need to eat."

"I'll eat." Tonight. Maybe. I need to diet before I get naked in front of Mr. Men's Magazine Muscle Model 1 and 2.

"What will you eat?"

Gah, the questions. "A salad?"

"With?"

"With chicken?"

"And?"

"And a breath mint?"

A low grumble tells me this is the wrong answer.

"All right, all right, I'll get a salad and half a sandwich." A salad won't fill me anyway.

"Good girl," he says. "I'll call you tonight."

I hang up, a bit bemused. Did he call me to crow about his conquest, and spend the whole time interrogating me on my eating habits? It should be overbearing but it isn't.

It's like he actually cares about me. I shake my head and get busy ordering my food.

After my sandwich I do feel better. With a full stomach stabilizing me, I put my head down and plow through work.

When I pick my head up, I'm rewarded with a Sawyer text.

How was the carnival?

Great. I had an epic freak out and Bear kissed it better. I do not share this.

You owe me.

What? I resist the urge to add seven exclamation points.

Pregame. Bear got his. I get a turn.

Right. Because it's a competition. And Bear definitely got his.

Okay. How much did Bear tell Sawyer about our Ferris wheel moment? *What are we going to do?*

I'm thinking... baseball. Or do you prefer tennis?

Fuck. Bear told him everything.

PREGAME WITH SAWYER is a picnic in a park.

"Bear says you have to eat more than one bite." Sawyer lays out a small platter of olives, cheese, hummus.

"He's so bossy."

"Yeah, well, get used to that."

I grab a cracker and dig in.

"Tennis," Sawyer nods to the courts nearby. I shake my head. I knew I was going to regret this.

I crunch cucumber slices and watch the tennis players until Sawyer throws an olive at me. "Whatcha thinking?"

"Is it true you compete in everything?"

Sawyer shrugs. "It was true in high school. After graduation, he focused on building his business and I traveled the surfing circuit."

"What made you come back?"

"Who says I'm back? I go where the waves take me." He flops back on the blanket, close enough his blond locks spill along my leg. I stroke a silky strand.

"You and Bear seems so different. You're a free spirit and Bear is so grounded." Like a mountain.

"We have enough in common. Our taste in women."

I roll my eyes.

After our picnic, we stroll down a busy street.

"Evie," Sawyer grabs my hand to pull me to a stop. The sign above our heads reads *Taboo.*

Gulp. We're in front of a sex shop.

Sawyer raises a brow in a silent dare. The old Evie would protest and blush to the roots of her hair. I stride towards the shop.

Sawyer catches up in time to open the door. I smile coolly and glide past him as if I do this every day. Until I see the wall of vibrators and halt.

Sawyer strolls past me, hands in his pockets. He peruses the garish display like he's a spectator at an art museum. "So," he says, "What's your pleasure?"

"Seriously?"

"It'll be good to know what you're into." He waggles his brows. "See anything you like?"

My eyes snag on a bright purple dildo covered in knobs. The end forks into two. Why so many prongs?

"Maybe," I breeze into a second, smaller room and grind to a halt. Metal studded leather covers the walls. Leashes, whips, paddles… I reach out and caress a wicked looking crop, unable to stop myself.

Sawyer makes a curious noise between a gurgle and a groan. His eyes are pools of pure lust.

"I'm curious," I offer, tracing my finger over a ball gag. "If I wanted to try something like this…"

"Forget the competition. I'm kidnapping you to my sex dungeon right now."

"You have a sex dungeon?" I can't hide my excitement.

"No but give me an hour." He makes a show of looking around the room. "I'll max my credit card and make one."

I show him a strap on, complete with image of a domme and hooded man on his knees. "Maybe I'm the one who wants to do the kidnapping."

"I'm down if you are."

I pretend to consider this, continuing to explore. I can't believe I haven't dissolved into a gooey puddle.

A rack of bulb-like items makes me pause. Some are metal, some silicone, others have jewels on the end.

"What are—" my eyes widen when I read the name on the tag.

"Have you tried buttstuff?"

I shake my head.

"Do you want to?"

"I'll try anything once."

He groans. "I need a moment. You win this round."

When I leave the room, he's buying something.

"What...?" I reach for the bag and he grabs it away.

"You'll find out. If you're good."

I thread my arm through his. "You like me bad." It is official. I am a different Evie around these guys.

"Ice cream?" he asks after we've walked half a block.

"Not for me."

Just like that, my bravado vanishes. I can't eat dessert in front of this hot guy. Everyone is already going to wonder why he's with the fat girl.

Without arguing, he buys a cone and leads me down the street. He catches my hand with his free one and squeezes. We're well past the shops, closer to the city baseball stadium when he pulls me into the shadows near a wall.

"Your ice cream is melting," I warn him.

He tilts his head and runs his tongue around the melty scoop. Oh, yes, I am jealous.

"Help me," he tilts the cone my way, and I lean in, catching the cream on my tongue. He tugs me closer so we both can work on the cone at the same time.

Lick. Lick. Any second our tongues will meet.

Light explodes above our head and I jump.

"Easy," He puts his arm around me. "Just the fireworks. They always do this first game of the season." A whistle and another burst of red and blue light.

Without thinking, I lean into Sawyer's warm, strong body and his arms come around me. Fireworks dazzling the sky, rich cream on my tongue, and a hot guy holding me equals a perfect night. Sawyer's the type of guy I would lust after in high school but never dare talk to. I couldn't brave the crowds of cheerleaders surrounding him, lest I be laughed off for not being thin and perky enough. Tonight, it's easy to be with him, easier than I thought it would be.

It's just a game.

I let my head fall back on his shoulder, my body relaxing into his. My booty brushes his groin and Sawyer growls in my ear.

"Evie." He turns me to him and grips my chin, holding me in place. Fire flowers bloom in the sky as he slants his head and kisses the hell out of me. Heat rolls up my legs, tingles the tips of my breasts. Sawyer's lips move over mine, his tongue licking like I'm ice cream about to melt. And I am melting. I grab his shoulders and hang on for dear life.

He breaks the kiss. For a moment we're silent, chests heaving together.

"That was..." I touch my numbed lips.

"Great," Sawyer says with satisfaction. He turns me back to the light show, holding me against his body. My nerves sing.

"Sawyer," I whisper, but he interrupts, breaking the spell.

"Now Bear and I are even."

"How was your night with Sawyer?" It's a few days after my pregame excursion with Sawyer. I'm sitting on my couch with the TV on silent, talking to Bear. He's taken to calling me every night while Sawyer and I text all day. I don't want to admit how much I look forward to Bear's gravelly voice on the other end of the phone, even if he's always so serious. Sawyer is flirtier.

I touch my lips where I still feel the ghost of Sawyer's kiss. He'd swept me off my feet until I floated in the sky with the fireworks. It wasn't his fault I forgot it was a game. The moment he reminded me; I came crashing down.

"Amazing. You and he are even." There. My voice is coy

and flirty, not a hint of wobble to betray my raw, unsure feelings. Which is crazy. I shouldn't have feelings. I take a deep breath and change the subject. "We visited a sex shop."

"He told me." The pure liquid heat in Bear's voice scatters my uncertainty. I sit up.

"He did?" I purr. "What did he tell you?"

"Enough to confirm you're everything we wanted and more."

I sink back on the couch, chest heaving. Close to climaxing from his smooth compliment. Being wanted is the best aphrodisiac.

"Before we start, we need to discuss the terms."

"The terms?"

"The terms of the competition. We each get three chances with you, alone." I note he doesn't use the 'd' word. This definitely isn't about dating me. "If you don't decide the winner by then, there'll be a final round."

"Okay." I'm glad I'm on the phone. Eventually I'll stop blushing at the thought of being with them. Maybe. After three rounds each, I'll be cool, worldly and sophisticated. Ready to jump into bed with a hot guy, no strings attached. No messy emotions tangled up inside.

"Talking by phone or text doesn't count as a round. It's best if we get to know each other as much as possible. You gotta be comfortable with us." He pauses. "You gonna be able to do this?"

"Yes." I am cool and calm as a movie star on the red carpet. Everyone wants a piece of me. I stand resilient in the endless stream camera flashes.

I'll play this role while they play their games.

"Good luck." I tell him graciously, then rethink it. Maybe this is like theater, where wishing someone good luck is bad luck. "Break a leg. Or a dick." Gah, that doesn't sound right.

"There's more," he says after a pause, during which I berate myself for being the most awkward person ever. "We have some rules."

"Rules. Like... no rebounds?" I smirk at my own sporty joke.

"Rules for you."

I sit up straighter, not sure what to say.

"Some of them you'll learn as we go. But if you agree to this, there's one you need to know now. As long as we're doing this, you don't come."

"I thought the point was for me to orgasm."

"You will. But not without permission."

"So when I'm alone..."

"You can ask permission. We may or may not say yes. And when you're with us, you ask. Every time." His voice is dead serious.

"You assume I'll be able to orgasm."

"I know you will."

"Okay, fine. I'll ask permission." A little heat flares in my pussy. Apparently, I like this stipulation. Weird. "Any other rules you want to tell me?"

"That's it for now. You ready to do this?"

I take a deep breath. I'm a suave, sophisticated woman, about to embark on an affair with a pair of men. It's like *Sex in the City* without the great shoes. "You had me at *hello*. Or, in this case, *orgasm*."

"Good, baby. Then it starts now." His voice deepens. "Where are you?"

"On the couch, watching TV."

"Turn it off," he orders.

Bemused, a little curious why I'm obeying, I do.

"Are you wearing clothes?"

"Yeah, what I wear to bed. Shorts and a t-shirt."

"You live with anyone? Roommates, baby," he clarifies when I hesitate.

"No."

"Take off the shorts. From now on you sleep in just a t-shirt."

I swallow. "Okay."

His voice changes again, becoming gentle. "You doing okay?"

"Uh, yeah." I do a mental checkup. My body tingles with excitement.

"If I tell you to do something you don't want to, just talk to me, okay?"

"Okay."

"Good, baby," he croons and warmth spreads through me. "Now, put me on speaker." He waits until I confirm, then orders, "Take off your panties."

Oh God. Oh God. My hands shake a little as I strip down.

"Get comfortable on the couch and keep your legs open."

I obey, panting a little. I feel wired, alive, like I've entered a new dimension. "Bear?"

"Yeah, baby?"

"Nothing. Never mind." Lying back, I let my legs flop open. The only way I could be more charged with excitement is if a portal opened up in front of my TV and he appeared to watch me.

Oh God. I was going to orgasm from him just telling me what to do.

"You know what comes next, right?" His voice is low, heady. It hits my bloodstream like alcohol. "Touch yourself."

"Fuck," I breathe.

"No swearing. Another rule."

My breath gusts out in a laugh. "I can't swear?"

"Or else face the consequences."

"What consequences?" Now I'm really curious.

"Disobey and find out. Are you touching?"

My fingers slide against my sweet spot, my flesh growing wetter by the second. "Yeah."

"Talk to me. Tell me how you get off."

Oh God. "I touch, um, myself."

"On your clit?"

"Near it. Kinda above it. Light strokes." My voice slurs like I'm drunk.

"Are you wet, baby?"

Baby. I don't know why it gets me, but it does. "Yes."

"If I was there, I'd make you show me." My fingers quicken at the tortured gravel of his voice. "I'd make you spread your legs wider and show me everything." My legs automatically slide apart further. The angle sparks new pleasure and my breath catches. "That's it, keep stroking. From now on you only touch when I give you permission, understand?"

"Ah, um, okay." I'm in no position to formulate a logical argument.

"Are you close?"

"Yes." I haven't been this turned on before when touching myself. Maybe ever.

"Keep going. Tell me when you're right on the edge."

He gets quiet, but his voice, the mental picture of him waiting, watching, dictating my every move drives my pleasure. I touch myself by his leave. Each stroke brings me closer to him and the tipping point.

"Okay. I'm close." My fingers speed up, grasping for the orgasm hovering just out of reach.

"Stop."

I make a sound like "nuh", but he ignores it.

"That was good, baby. You did good. Now go to sleep."

My pussy pulses in protest. "What? You don't want me to come?"

"Not tonight."

"Damn," I say, and belatedly remember his earlier instruction. "I mean, darn."

"Will you be able to sleep?"

"Eventually," I manage, and he chuckles.

"Text me in the morning."

"Okay." It's insane how he orders me about and I just... melt.

I hang up, feeling like I can do this. Whatever game he's playing, it's working for me.

~

"You close, baby?" Bear's voice heavy in my ear. Fingers strum my clit, making music of my moans. My hips rise, my toes curling. I'm wet and tight and ready. "You're close," he mutters with satisfaction and when he slides two thick fingers inside my channel, I begin to shake...

My phone buzzes on my nightstand and I jerk awake. My orgasm rises like a ghost above my bed and slips away. My pussy throbs.

Oh my God. The first sex dream of my life and I almost came. I grab my phone and click off my alarm. My legs wobble as I stagger to the bathroom. My cheeks are flushed, my nipples peaked. What is happening to me?

In the shower, I glide my hands over my wet skin. The memory of Bear's voice echoes in the small space, vibrating deep in my pussy. I prop my leg on the tub edge and slide a finger over my pussy...

From now on you only touch when I give you permission.

Shit. I mean, *poop*. I have rules now.

Pussy pulsing, I hurry and finish cleaning up, dashing to my phone. He told me to text him.

Morning. I type quickly and send.

His reply is immediate. Was he waiting for me?

Morning, baby. How'd you sleep?

Once I settled down, I dropped right off. *Really well. I had a dream. It worked me up. A good dream*. I clarify.

Did you touch?

In the shower. But I stopped! I'm hunched over the phone, towel sagging, hair dripping on my wood floor, waiting for his verdict.

Good girl.

Why do those two words mean so much? I'm happy and relieved enough to feel cheeky. *So I'm not in trouble?* I chuckle to myself as I poke the Bear.

Do you want to be?

I squirm and drop the phone. I should get ready for work.

But when I return to my phone, heels clicking on my wood floor, the question is still waiting. I like being a 'good girl' but what if I was naughty?

Maybe. Will you punish me?

With pleasure.

My nipples pop, clearly visible through my bra and blouse. This is a new dimension to the game.

Text me when you get to work, he orders, and dang if the command doesn't my make nipples throb. My pussy clenches, begging for relief. How am I going to survive until the competition starts?

~

This is so unfair! I vent one day to Sawyer by text.

What?

Bear keeps winding me up with no release. I feel like a toy!

Is that a bad thing?

I consider. *No, it's kinda hot.*

He sends a smiling demon emoji. I can almost hear his sinful chuckle.

Meanie.

You love it.

I hide my phone as my boss stalks by. I've taken to getting to the office early and blowing through my work before noon. Sawyer usually texts me after lunch and once he does, it's a miracle if I get anything done.

Seriously, why is Bear so bossy?

He likes things a certain way.

No kidding. Today he made me take a picture of my lunch —before and after, so he could be sure I'd eaten enough. If I'm honest, his concern makes me feel good.

But our late-night talks culminating with me begging for orgasm and him denying me?

I'm dying, I text Sawyer. *I won't make it a week.* The competition starts Thursday. *I'll explode.*

That's fine, as long as you do it on my face.

Guhhhh. Is that an order?

Yes.

I made a mistake raising the stakes in the sex shop.

"Bear, please," I beg that night in bed, the phone pressed against my ear and my hands shaking above my pussy, obedient to his order to stop. "Please, please, please."

"Patience, baby."

"But—"

"Good night. Remember to text me in the morning."

"How could I forget?" I mutter and roll over to groan into

the pillow. These men are my days and my nights, the first thing on my mind in the morning and the last thing at night. I am a volcano of sexual need, counting the hours and minutes and seconds to our eventual sexy time, my own personal "Cum-mageddon."

Finally, the day arrives.

CHAPTER 4

ROUND 1

Bear pulls up in a bright yellow Hummer. It's been over a week since the carnival and he's bigger than I remember. Good thing he offered to drive—there's no way my Civic would fit his massive frame.

He comes around to open my door. He has to give me a boost, and he lifts me like I weigh nothing, his hands fitting easily around my waist. He buckles me in like I'm five. His big hand slides down my leg before he shuts my door, leaving every nerve ending in me on high alert.

"Hungry?" Bear asks as he pulls into traffic. I wipe my hands on my jeans. *Dress casual*, he told me.

He notices my nervousness. "You don't have anything to be worried about."

"That's right. All the pressure is on you."

"Exactly. You just relax and do what I tell you."

Ngghhh. I slide down a little in the seat. Don't know why, but I get really horny whenever he says stuff like that.

"I figured we could have dinner at my place," he says casually, and now I know the location of Cum-maggedon. His place.

"But first, an errand." He pulls into the mall.

I sit up.

"You need a dress for your cousin's wedding."

"You're kidding me." I may have complained about my dress hunting chore one too many times, but I didn't expect this. "You're offering moral support?"

"I'm up for a fashion show." He puts the Hummer in park and comes around to open my door.

My feet drag as we pass a Victoria Secret store, the giant picture of an underwear model blowing a kiss in her skivvies increasing my own feelings of dread.

"Do we have to? Can't we just get a slushie and then go to your place?" How did I end up with the only guy in the world who likes to shop?

I tug on Bear's hand, but there's no escaping a guy who's six four and works out five hours a day. He strolls into the department store, right up to saleslady.

"My girl needs a dress."

The saleslady blinks up at him. I hang back, hoping she doesn't recognize me.

"What's the occasion?"

"Attending a wedding."

"Not black then," she says before I can open my mouth. She heads full steam for the dress section, snatching selections off the rack, with Bear and I in tow.

He is serious about the fashion show. I strip and dress in record time, and promenade past him, carefully avoiding looking in mirrors. Bear keeps his arms crossed over his chest, biceps bulging, totally macho even surrounded by floral prints. His face is impassive, but I catch a shimmer of interest when I emerge in royal blue.

"Lovely," the saleslady breathes. The fabric of the dress molds to my torso, accenting my waist before flaring at the hips.

"It's too tight at the top." I pick at the skirt, which is full and swirly.

"Nonsense," she says. "You have a perfect hourglass figure. You should show it off. A whiff of cleavage isn't bad." She winks.

Not so much a whiff as an endless chasm. I avoid glancing down in case I get vertigo.

"And the blue matches your eyes," the lady trills. As if anyone's gonna be looking anywhere but at the cleavage chasm.

"Perfect," Bear rumbles. "We'll take it."

My mouth drops open, but I don't have a choice. The look he's leveling at me is new, but I read it perfectly. *Just relax and do what I tell you.*

I change back and head to the cashier, figuring I can always return the dress later, but Bear already has his credit card out. Before I can protest, he's paid and secured the dress bag on his arm, me on the other, and we're walking out of the store.

"One more stop." He guides me towards the giant poster of the underwear model. Pulling me towards...

Oh no. Oh no.

"No, no, no," I say, tugging against Bear's grip. His big hand clamps around my wrist, gentle but strong as a lock.

"Why not?"

"Why not?" I wave at the sky-high underwear model. Blown up to cover the side of the building, this woman is a modern goddess, inviting worship. You'd think you'd be able to find some little mark of imperfection, but no. Just flawless skin. Cheekbones for days. Who can compete?

"Come on," he says before I can sputter excuses about voyeuristic consumers and objectification. The truth is, I avoided a total breakdown in one dressing room, but there's no way my luck will extend to two.

Bear pulls me into the store. Everywhere is a sexy woman made of cardboard, giving us 'bedroom eyes' above mounds of pink and black lace.

"Pick something out," his order is a hot whisper in my ear, "or I will."

In a daze, I pivot, arms out like a zombie, and grab two handfuls of polyester. Sales ladies cluster around Bear's big form, their hearts in their eyes. He sends them scurrying to all corners of the store, and I end up in a dressing room, buried under bra and undie sets.

"Your boyfriend is so attentive," one lady tells me as she hands over Bear's selections. I turn into a tomato, round and red. At least he doesn't ask me to model for him.

I say yes to his choices, if only to get out of the dressing room sooner. Once again, he pays and collects the bags.

"You don't like shopping?" he asks as I cringe past the picture of the giant model outside the store.

"Not really. I'm fat."

His eyes narrow, but he doesn't say anything until we're in the car.

"Time for another rule."

I nod, my heart tripping in my chest.

He jerks his head toward the bags in the back. "Before you dress in the morning, you text me a picture."

"A picture?" I ask, heat racing across my chest. Something tells me he doesn't want a picture of my bedhead.

"Yeah, baby. You send me pictures of you wearing two different panties. I'll decide which one you'll wear, if I allow panties that day."

I blink, then realize he's said something else. I lost it for the moment there, somewhere in the haze of lust and bewilderment. "Um, what?"

His voice takes on a sterner edge. "Pay attention, baby. Did you understand your instruction?"

I nod.

He smiles. "And you already understand that not following my instructions means there will be consequences."

It's not a question, but a statement. The way my body flames at this, I have a feeling I might like his "consequences."

"Mhm," I manage to eke out, not trusting my voice.

Then we're pulling into a numbered parking space in front of a townhome. Bear ushers me in with a hand on my back, unlocking the door and letting me go first. His place is clean with a faint citrus scent. The open floor plan has a sunken living room with two steps leading to a dining area where a black table is laid with six places. Beyond that a bar with tall black chairs separates the eating area from the kitchen.

Bear plants me on the couch in front of the giant TV, fixes me a drink, and starts rummaging around the kitchen while I sit. Is there anything more attractive than a man who wants to feed me?

There's nothing less attractive than a woman who eats too much. Auntie Jen's voice scolds when I'm halfway through my meal.

"I should eat less," I say, and then berate myself. The only thing less attractive than fat is talking constantly about needing to lose it.

"You're fine, baby." Bear works steadily through his own plate. "You'll need the calories."

I shiver at the promise. Bear is so big; I could comfortably sit in his lap. He'd be a living, breathing, muscly armchair. After we watch a movie, I could turn around and I'd be in the perfect position to ride...

"So, you work out a lot?" I eye his t-shirt, the fabric stretched tight over his pecs. "'Cause it's working."

He grins. There's a hint of a dimple in his right cheek.

I put a hand to my belly. "I need to work out more."

"I can help with that." His hand curls around my neck. "Stick around." He plays with a lock of my hair for a moment before leaning close. His lips brush my ear. "I'll work you real good."

My heart seizes and I freeze, waiting for him to follow through, but he pulls away, stacking our plates.

I follow him to the kitchen on unsteady legs, lingering at the bar while he loads the dishes in the dishwasher.

Three dates each. Essentially a six-night stand. But there's a garment bag and three Victoria Secret bags in the backseat of his Hummer that speak for something more serious. Why is he going through all this trouble?

He likes things a certain way, Sawyer said. It won't kill me to go along with his rules. If I had to admit it, I like the way he takes control. My ex and I couldn't even decide where to go for dinner, and when I insisted he pick because I was mentally exhausted after work, he got all sulky.

I realize that Bear is leaning against the bar, studying me with a slight wrinkle in his brow. "You're really caught up in your head."

"Yeah."

"It's okay, baby. You can let go."

"I don't know how to do that. Except, I guess, at the bar. I was pretty loose then." And look how that turned out.

He reaches down and grasps my hips, lifting me on to the barstool. I squawk and flail a little.

"Shh, baby, I've got you." He props me up easily. "Just relax."

"Oh, right, just relax. Why didn't I think of that?" It's starting. Cum-mageddon. It's finally happening.

Shiver.

"I want to try a little experiment."

"O-kay." I don't point out that this whole endeavor is highly experimental. For me anyway.

His big hand comes to the back of my neck, kneading gently. "While we're together, I want you to obey me."

"Obey you? Like... in bed?" He certainly hasn't had an issue ordering me around so far. Maybe he's been easing me into it.

"I think it might work for us."

Us? There's an us?

He must've read my question on my face because he amends. "It'll help you. You need to switch off your brain so you can have a good time."

"I need to get out of my frontal and temporal lobe," I parrot an article I'd read, when I was researching what's wrong with me. "Women need to switch off to have an orgasm."

"There you go," he says, and I realize I've given him scientific proof that he's right.

"How do you know it will work?"

"It's worked so far for you? The rules?"

"Yeah. I guess so. I now have a dress to wear to the wedding." I shift on the stool and consider it. Turn off for a night and just go with the flow? Tempting. Very tempting.

"Are you okay with it? Taking over?" It feels like he'll be doing all the work.

A flash of white teeth. "Oh, yes, baby. I am very much okay with it."

"All right," I shrug.

"First things first." His hands roam down my neck and shoulders, squeezing away tension, "No more saying mean things about yourself."

"But—"

"I mean it. If a guy said those things about you, I'd punch him in the face." He looks so intense I almost recoil, but the way he's running his hands up and down my arms is so soothing.

"I don't say anything mean about myself. It's all true."

A sound breaks from his throat, low and angry. A growl.

It's a testament to how safe I feel with him that I ignore it. "What have I said mean about myself?"

"You called yourself fat."

"I am fat."

Another growl. His big hands curl over my shoulders and squeeze lightly.

"I mean, I have fat on my body," I babble.

"That's not what you mean. The way you say it, it means 'ugly.'"

Tears prick my eyes. "Yeah."

"Baby." His voice softens. "Look at me. You have the body of a pinup girl. You think this," he smooths down my shirt alongside my breasts, "and this," he grasps my hips, fingers digging into my ass, "isn't a turn on?"

"But—"

"I don't want to hear any more." He steps closer, drawing my legs around his waist. His forehead drops to mine and he murmurs, "You're so little."

"No, I'm not."

"You are to me."

I open my mouth and his brown eyes meet mine.

"Say it again. I dare you."

"Or else... consequences?"

"You got it."

"I'm a feminist," I tell him.

"So am I."

I make a little noise like "huh."

"I wholly admire and respect you as a person. You have a right to your body. My job," he squeezes my knee, "is to get you intrigued enough to give me consent."

"If I consent, then what happens?"

"I make it worth your while. Very, very worth it."

"You'd be the first," I say almost apologetically.

He grins and I get the feeling that he doesn't mind being the first. He seems the type who'd want to be first, last and only.

Except with me. This is just a game. I shake off any thought that I'm special.

"This is kinda kinky," I announce instead.

"It's whatever we want it to be. Do you like it?"

"Yeah."

"Good." He lifts me again, carrying me to the couch. I have to admit; I get a thrill from the easy way he handles me. This time he sits and has me straddle him. It's just as I imagined. Better.

Our lips touch and toy with each other. I twine my hands around his neck and press closer. He tastes like whiskey and with each sip, I grow more and more floaty. I lean back, realizing I've been rocking a little against his large frame. He grips my hips, pulling me against him and my whole body shivers.

His dimple deepens. "Remember not to come."

"I thought the whole point—"

"Without permission," he clarifies. "Remember?" He leans forward to get more of his drink, taking me with him. My body arches helplessly against his.

I pout. "So many rules."

"You like them."

To hide how close I am to losing control, I reach for my wine. The glass is empty, so I go for Bear's drink instead.

"No, no more booze. Don't want you drunk."

I roll my eyes. "Okay, dad."

Something flashes in his eyes. "Daddy."

"What?"

"Say it."

"Daddy?"

Something long and hard grows under me. My pussy clenches.

"You like that?" I ask, and add, in a breathy voice, "Daddy?"

"Mmmm," Bear rumbles. He turns us so I'm on the couch and he's kneeling. He splays a hand on my chest, guides me down on my back. "Good, baby. You earned a reward."

I quiver a little as he draws my jeans down. His fingers brush the front of my panties and I almost snap my legs back together.

"Holy fuck."

He squeezes my bottom and smacks it. "No swearing."

"Yes, daddy." If someone had told me a month ago I'd be getting sexed up on a couch by a hot guy and calling him daddy while he ordered me around, I would've assumed they were high. But now that I've surrendered, it's working for me. The commands, the 'daddy' game, all of it.

Another rumble, more like a growl. His big hands cup my bottom, and strip off my panties with expert speed. Then he's kneeling on the floor and propping my legs on his shoulders, splaying me open to his hot breath.

My head falls back as he nibbles up my thigh his big hands kneading my bottom.

"F...udge." I scramble. "Fork. Funky nassar."

"Shhhh. Let Daddy take of you."

Oh yes. Oh, that's hot.

My body melts into the couch. He teases me with little touches and his breath. I'm primed and ready. At the first lick, tingles shoot through me.

He slips a finger inside and stirs up more arousal. I can't help but rock a little on his fingers, silently begging for more. His finger slips down and teases my bottom hole.

Record scratch. I raise my head. "What are you doing?"

"Shh, baby." His finger, wet from my arousal, circles my back door. I don't want it to feel good, but it does. "Trust me."

"I..." My legs are quivering, useless. I feebly kick a little.

"Be still," he says, and my body relaxes into the order. He holds me in thrall with a finger at my back entrance and thumb brushing my clit. His tongue takes another tour and little sounds escape my throat. My legs flex, electricity gathering at the base of my spine.

"Don't come," he raises his head long enough to warn.

"But—"

"No."

It's not fair. Every time he tells me not to come, my body slides a little closer. His fingers are magic, shooting sparks. His tongue dominates me until all I can think about is how great his cock will eventually feel. His cock—

My pussy clamps around his fingers. The arousal from

all those nights he worked me up and didn't let me get relief presses on me, threatening to come crashing down.

"You're being so good for me." His breath caresses my pussy between kisses and teasing licks. "You're my good girl. You earned a reward."

My orgasm is a bright light in the distance, rushing towards me, blinding. When it finally hits me, I'll be wrecked.

He whispers right into my pussy, "Daddy's gonna take care of you."

I make a noise like "nuuuh."

"Come, baby," he orders, and my mind goes white. Far, far below, my body bucks and shudders.

He works me with his fingers and tongue, as I mewl and sigh, legs twitching, toes curling. Pleasure ebbs over me, sapping all my strength. As I lay there, panting, he kisses my thigh.

"Good girl."

My head rolls on the pillow, and I fix on the hard bar pressing against his jeans. I reach for it and he catches my hand.

"Not tonight. This was all about you."

I'm too spent to speak. He leaves, returns with a cloth and cleans me, then gathers me against him. I curl into his giant frame like I was fitted for it. Arms locked around me, smooth, warm muscle under my cheek. Large hands splayed over my back. The only thing out of place is the telltale ridge under my bottom. But I'll think about that tomorrow.

This is just the beginning.

CHAPTER 5

ROUND 2

"I HAVE to text him every morning and wait for him to text back," I complain to Sawyer, breaking another one of Auntie Jen's cardinal rules of dating: when out with a guy, don't talk about another guy. But these guys don't follow Auntie Jen's rules, so why should I?

"But you agreed to it," he points out. "And you haven't disobeyed." His hair blows around his handsome face as he pulls into the beach lot. He parks and leans close. "Methinks the lady doth protest too much." He tucks a stray hair behind my ear and taps my nose before slipping from the car.

After my night with Bear, I almost cancelled the competition. He made me come in about two minutes—wasn't that the point of all this? I could just give the winner trophy to Bear, so did we really need to continue?

The fact that I'd be crushed with disappointment shouldn't be a factor. It'd only be worse if I played along for the whole month.

When I texted Sawyer that I had a good time, he responded, "You ain't seen nothing yet."

I couldn't call things off after that. I was too intrigued.

Sawyer pauses a moment in front of the car, hand shielding his eyes as he looks over the beach, and I study him. He picked me up in his dirty Jeep, blond hair tousled from the windy ride. Flip flops, board shorts hanging off his lean hips, and no shirt. He's not as big as Bear, but who is? Sawyer's body is a tanned masterpiece, his chest and abs a perfect wall of muscle. He should be running down the beach with a bikini model, *Baywatch* style. Not here with me.

"Evie," Sawyer calls. I blink and realize he's holding my door open.

"Sorry," I take his hand and scramble out. He's just like Bear—opening my door. He buckled me in earlier, too.

"You got that look," he says.

"What look?"

"The one Bear talks about. You're thinking shit about yourself."

"What? Am not," I lie automatically. I can't believe they talk about me. It makes me nervous and excited at the same time.

"Can't lie to me." He grabs a blanket and hands me a large water bottle. "Bear's super good at this intuitive stuff. He should open up a shrink office next to the body shop. People can get their heads fixed with their oil change."

"What, really?" I imagine Bear manning a lemonade stand with a sign: *Psychiatric Help, five cents.*

"Oh yeah," Sawyer says. "All those guys getting fancy

rims or racing stripes are just insecure about relating to women. Or something." He shrugs. "He loves helping people through their problems. Next to fixing and pimping cars, it's his favorite project."

Ah. Great. So I'm a project. "So what about me?" I ask breezily. "Do I have daddy issues?"

He grins. "You do now. You okay with that term?"

I shrug. "Do you like it?"

"Not as much as Bear. But yeah, it works for me." He holds out his hand. "Ready?"

I take it. I'll be all right. I'm dressed in shorts and a t-shirt. A sports bra.

"No bikini?" he asks.

I shrug. He grins and shakes his head. If he tells Bear, I'll probably end up on another shopping trip.

"So why'd you bring me here?" I look down the beach. A few women are lying out, gleaming with oil. One waves to Sawyer and I turn away before I see his response.

"Ever been surfing?" he asks.

"No... we're not going to do that, are we?"

He chuckles. "Maybe next time. You'd look great in a wetsuit."

I roll my eyes.

"Come on. I wanna show you something."

We head down past the pier. The beach gets more and more deserted the closer we get to the bluffs. When we get there, we start to climb, taking long draws on the water bottle as the sun beats down.

We reach an overlook and stop to take in the view, passing the water bottle back and forth.

"It's a wildlife sanctuary." Sawyer nods to the abandoned stretch of beach between two cliffs. White birds dot the sands.

"It's gorgeous."

"You're gorgeous," Sawyers says, and pulls me against him, back to front. His hands go to my waist and smooth up and down. "The way you curve... fuck. This t-shirt is a crime."

Biting my lip, I step away. I tug off the shirt and face him only wearing my sports bra. "Better?"

"Fuck yes." He comes in close again, head slanted for a kiss.

Our lips meet and it's all sweet and delicate, a camera-ready kiss with the ocean and sky as the backdrop. Then his tongue starts to toy with me, and I answer the challenge, dueling slyly as the world fades away. My hands take the opportunity to slide over his sleek muscle, exploring the flex of his arms as he tugs me close, the rise and fall of his chest and back as he makes promises with his mouth only his body can keep.

Someone coughs and we jerk apart. A skinny man stares at us, his Adam's apple bobbing up and down. He's holding binoculars.

"What the fuck, man?" Sawyer barks, and the man jumps, almost dropping the binoculars. He looks mortified.

"Birdwatching. Sorry," he scuttles away.

"Fuck," Sawyer mutters again but makes no move to touch me until the guy is out of sight. I giggle.

"You think it's funny?" There's a dangerous glint in Sawyer's eyes. He maneuvers me back behind a boulder, out of sight.

"A little."

"You like an audience?"

I shrug. "Isn't that why you brought me up here? To get a thrill?"

"Fuck me," he comes at me again. "You naughty, naughty girl."

"You're supposed to make me come," I whisper as he kisses my mouth, my neck, the hinge of my jaw.

"What about these?" he tugs at my shorts.

"What about them?"

He smiles slyly as his hands dip under the waistband of my shorts. "What color is your underwear?"

"Why don't you ask Bear?" I sass back. "He chose them."

"Fuck me," Sawyer groans. "I wanna be your daddy. Call me Daddy, too."

"Okay, Daddy Two." I hold up two fingers. "If you want to be number one, you gotta earn it." It is a competition. I figure the more competitive these guys get, the more I win.

"Naughty," he growls, and tugs at my shorts. "Lose these."

"What if Mr. Birdwatcher comes back?"

Sawyer raises a wicked eyebrow.

I lean back against the rock, realizing his body will block any sight of me.

"All right," I whisper, and let him remove my shorts.

"Blue," he says at the sight of my hip huggers.

"Like your eyes," I tell him, and get a smile.

"They almost look like bikini bottoms." He eyes me up and down and I realize I'm essentially wearing a bathing suit.

He bundles up my shorts and t-shirt and pretends to toss them out over the cliff.

"No!" I cry, tackling him. We wrestle a moment and my clothes end up draped on a nearby bush. Sawyer holds my wrists.

"Do you trust me?"

"No."

His teeth flash white as he laughs. “Come on, baby. Live a little.”

I sigh. “All right, yes.”

“Yes what?”

“Yes, daddy.”

“Fuck, that is hot. Come here and let daddy take care of you.”

He arranges me near the overlook, my back to his front, facing the ocean. We’re just behind the boulders, so anyone coming up the path can’t see our bodies. If a birdwatcher returns, it’ll look like we’re just taking in the view, cuddling like a couple with Sawyer’s arms around me. They won't see his hand down my panties.

One long finger stirs against my sweet spot. “You like this?”

“The view? Oh yes, it’s nice.”

His chuckle gusts in my ear. I gently grind my bottom against him in response to the swirl of his fingers.

“Just relax. I’ve got you.” Sawyer kisses my neck and sucks a little. I sigh, letting my head rest against his chest. He sucks harder. My knees buckle and he takes my weight, holding me up.

“Bear doesn’t allow you to come without asking permission.”

“That’s... right,” I marshal my thoughts against the distracting flutter of his fingers.

“So, what would you do if I stopped?” His finger stills.

My breath hisses. “I’d be upset.”

His jaw moves along my cheek. “How upset?”

“Really mad.”

“But you couldn’t do anything about it.” His arms flex around me.

"You gonna keep me up here forever?" A seagull swoops below us, hovering over the breaking waves.

"Maybe. What will you do if I let you go?"

"I'll find that birdwatcher guy," I answer tartly. His finger makes a tiny movement and my body strains towards his touch. "Maybe he'll make me come."

"Or you'll go get yourself off."

"Good idea." I try to move my hips and his arms clamp down, keeping me still.

"Maybe I should tie you up." My body clenches. Sawyer feels it. "You like that? Bear was right."

"What?"

"You need someone else to take control."

"No."

"Yep. That's what you need to get off."

I slump a little. He's right. "So?"

"So it's up to me if you get off right now."

"Sawyer," I start to whine.

"Ask nicely."

"Please, daddy," I say in a breathy, Marilyn Monroe voice. "Make me come?"

"Good girl. I'll think about it."

I squirm and he holds me tighter, his arms like iron bands. Arousal flows through me, hot and liquid, pooling at my core. My pussy pulses under the weight. His finger flutters against my clit, increasing the pressure.

"Keep that up and I'll come," I inform him breathlessly.

"Better not or you'll be punished."

"You wouldn't."

"Try me."

All this talk of punishment gives me a thrill. "What is it with you and Bear denying me?" I pout. "You're supposed to be doing the opposite."

"This is more fun." He slides his fingers in my folds, and pleasure pulses through me. I pant, pressing against his hand to get the stimulation I need.

"Please," I beg.

"What will I get if I let you?"

"Points. All the points."

"Tempting," he murmurs in my ear. "I do want to win." His voice hardens as he commands, "I'm your number one daddy. Say it."

"You're number one. Daddy... I can't—" My body moves restlessly against him. The vast ocean vista before me blurs.

"Kiss me," he commands and angles my head toward him. We're Jack and Rose on the bow of the Titanic. His mouth dominates me, his tongue thrusting until my pussy squeezes in sympathy, begging silently to be filled. I writhe against him, little noises breaking from my throat. Every last thought leaves my brain, helpless against the onslaught. The world falls away.

"Come, Evie," Sawyer breaks the kiss long enough to give the order. My cries break against the rocks below. Sawyer kisses me again as a flock of birds startle and fly in an undulating curve over the surf.

"I HEAR YOU NEED A BIKINI," Bear says when I traipse into Ballers after work the next day. We all agreed to meet and hang out.

I glare at Sawyer. "You have a big mouth,"

"The better to eat you with, my dear," the blond winks.

Bear leans into my space. "Do we need another trip to Victoria's Secret?"

"No." Not another. The first trip, I nearly died.

"Evie," he strokes the back of my neck in a way that makes me shiver. "I'll make it worth your while."

I raise a brow.

"Bear has a hot tub," Sawyer says, setting a drink in front of me.

"Do you?" I swivel to face the big man and his arms slip around me. It feels so good.

"Mhm," he rumbles.

"Then I'll just have to get a bathing suit." The world really is ending if I just volunteered to go shopping for swimwear.

"You won't regret it." Sawyer grabs my hand and plants a kiss on my knuckles. So chivalrous. Then he licks them. *Unf.*

Laughing, he drops my hand. Bear rests a hand on my back as Sawyer and I continue to flirt. The night unspools easily, me and them and them and me. What shape does our relationship make? What sort of geometry? A triangle, a circle around me with them in orbit—or do I orbit around them?

I lean back in my seat as Bear and Sawyer face the screens, arguing over some sport thing. I sip my drink and ponder, and I'm not the only one.

A woman in a suit leans down the bar in my direction, wide-eyed. Her gaze flicks from Bear's heights to Sawyer's blond crown. And me, I'm the valley between them. "Are you with... both of them?"

I grimace. "It's... complicated."

"WHY IS IT COMPLICATED?" Mina asks late that night.

"Me and two guys? Um, hello."

"So? You have enough orifices."

I sputter.

"Besides, you're overdue for a good fuck."

"Mina!"

"What?" Her voice is gilt with innocence. I know better. There's no innocence, just sin. "One of the guys you dated couldn't even find your vagina."

I grimaced, remembering. "He kept thrusting against my perineum."

"Ouch."

"Yeah. That is not an entry point, dude."

"Maybe you really are a virgin. Are you sure you've had sex?"

"Stop it."

"You stop overthinking things. You're making up for lost time."

"Maybe." I bite my lip.

"Are you worried that you're a slut? Because the 'slut' is a patriarchal construct to keep women from owning their sexuality. Punish women for behaving in a way that men do, behavior men are rewarded for."

"Right. Um, I'm not worried I'm a slut. I'm worried that I'm not worried... when I should be worried."

"My head hurts."

"Mine too."

"Why should you be worried?"

"I don't know," I hedge, even though I do. *Because this situation, this competition, this relationship isn't going to last.* I heave a sigh and check the time. "Crap, I've got to go. It's late."

"Whatever." Mina isn't impressed by my avoidance tactics.

"Isn't it like three am on the East Coast?"

"Yeah. Hey, I'm going to be busy the next few weeks. I'm moving to a new place. It's the bomb."

"Does anyone say that anymore? The bomb?"

"I just did. Night, bitch!"

I hang up and set my alarm, laughing to myself. Mina has the right attitude. Judge the competition, enjoy my orgasms until the time comes for me to leave. Get in, get off and go. *Thanks for the memories,* I imagine blowing a kiss to the guys and riding off into the sunset. In a convertible, not my little Civic. Maybe I can borrow Bear's car. Or buy one from him.

Either way, when I leave, I have a feeling I'll keep a piece of them. Just have to make sure they don't take everything from me.

The next morning I sleep through my alarm, and end up rushing around, rubbing sand from my eyes and digging through my closet for something that doesn't make me look like a Mennonite. I need more clothes that flatter my figure. Normally I'd shy away from that because my figure is so curvy, but just because my curves are bigger than most doesn't mean I should hide. Auntie Jen won't approve, but I'm not sleeping with her. I want to see Bear and Sawyer's eyes light up when I walk into a room, and if that means dressing sexy, so be it.

If the modest police stop me, I can tell them I'm playing sex games with two guys. My sexy qualifications are totally in order.

My phone alarm goes off again. *Crap. Almost forgot.*

I rush to text. *Daddy, can you pick my panties? There's blue, red, leopard print, nude...*

Put the blue ones on and show me.

Unf. *Okay, daddy.*

I snap a picture. A year ago, if you would've told me I'd

be taking pictures of my panty-clad behind willingly and texting them to one of the sexiest men alive, I would've laughed in your face before blushing so hard I spontaneously combusted.

Now red. I strip and comply. Whatever pair he does finally pick, I'll have to throw the other in the laundry basket.

Buzz goes my phone. *Red.*

Thank you, Daddy.

You're welcome, baby.

Then I go to work, panties already drenched.

"Do you realize what this ritual every morning does to me?" I ask when I've called to let him know I got to work safely.

"What, baby?" He knows. There's an edge of amusement to his tone.

I huff. "Asking you… makes me wet."

"That's the idea. Don't worry, I'll take care of you."

"When?" I demand.

He chuckles and tells me to have a good day.

I get through the morning with only two unwanted requests—both from my cousin. Even though I'm not in the wedding party, my cousin thinks it's fine to delegate tasks to me—picking up and mailing invitations, researching venues, interviewing caterers. I know I'm the boring, capable one, but seriously?

At least I have the next rounds with Bear and Sawyer to look forward to. Which gives me an idea...

For my lunch break, I head to the mall. I can't bring myself to go into Victoria's Secret, but they have bathing suits at the department store.

Except the second I close the dressing room door; I can't do this. The mirror dominates the space, reflecting back all my bulges and imperfections. Why did I subject myself to this? And what is the big deal? What is wrong with me that I can't even try on a bathing suit without judging myself?

My cell goes *brrrrt* with a text. Bear checking in to make sure I get lunch. *Have you eaten?*

I smile through my tears and stab the call button.

"Evie?"

"Hey," I can't hide the tears in my voice.

"Is something wrong? What is it? Did someone hurt you?"

His concern, intent with a dangerous edge, makes me smile.

"No," I wipe my eyes. "I'm in a dressing room." My voice breaks a little. "I thought I'd go shopping for a bathing suit. For you."

"Baby." His voice softens. "Are you alone?"

"Yeah. Just me and the mirror." *My nemesis.*

"What are you wearing?"

He's in bossy mode. I respond right away, grateful for something to focus on other than my own insecurities. "A skirt and a top. It's a little tight so I added a scarf."

"Take off your top."

"I can't." I avoid looking in the mirror. "I don't want to see myself."

"Baby," his voice is so gentle my heart breaks. "Do you trust me?"

"Yes."

"Yes?"

"Yes, Daddy."

"Raise the skirt." Back to bossy. Thank God. I need to turn my brain off right now. I wriggle the stretchy fabric up to my hips. "Okay, daddy."

"Spread your legs. Wide."

I rock back on the seat, lean against the wall and spread my knees as far as they can go. "Done."

"You're wearing your panties." He doesn't ask. He knows I am. He chose them this morning. "I want you to touch over the panties. Get yourself hot."

Oh boy. I stroke over the gusset, stirring a response almost immediately.

"Ooh..."

"Feel good, baby?"

"Yes, daddy," I whisper. "So good. I... I wish you were here."

"I do too." His deep voice curls around me, a warm blanket. "But it might be better that I'm not."

"We'd probably get arrested," I sigh into the phone. Bear couldn't sneak in here without being noticed by some pearl-clutching lady who was also a friend of my aunt's. But I imagine him here anyway—his broad shoulders filling my vision, big hand guiding mine to obey his commands. I sigh again and my head falls back against the wall. Pleasure swirls under my stroking fingers. If I brush too hard and too long in the right spot, I'll come.

"You wet?"

"You know I am," I keep my voice low.

"Stop touching and take off your top. Pull your bra down below your breasts. You can set the phone down."

I rush to obey. My bra is part of a lacy set. Since Bear took over my lingerie drawer, I can't bear to wear the giant utilitarian tank bras I used to solder on beneath my Mennonite chic clothes. When I pull the bra down below my breasts, they push up into snowy mounds. My breasts are pretty amazing. Twin Peaks of Perfection. The Eighth Wonder of the World.

I'm so pleased with the effect; I snap a picture and send

it to Bear. I put my phone to my ear and enjoy his rushed intake of breath.

"Like that?" I chuckle softly.

"Yes, baby. You're so beautiful. Your legs still spread?"

"Yes, daddy."

"Good. Go back to touching. Tell me when you're on the edge."

I go back to circling my clit through my damp panties. Oh, it's so good. Each brush of my fingertip pushes me closer, but I'm a good girl, so I stop when I'm about to tip over. "I'm here, daddy." Teetering on the edge.

"Is your hair down?"

I wrench out my ponytail holder and shake my mane loose over my shoulders. The auburn cascade frames my exposed chest.

"Touch your breasts. Pretend I'm touching them."

"Yes, daddy." My voice has that breathy little girl quality it gets when I'm really into a scene. I don't fight it.

"Do I make them feel good?"

"So good," I want to moan. If anyone comes into the dressing room, they're going to wonder what sort of clothes I'm trying on. *I'll have what she's having.* But they can't have my daddy. He's mine.

Bear's voice is a growl in my ear. "You touching yourself?"

I sneak one hand back between my legs while the other rubs over my chest. How did I not know massaging my breasts would feel this great? A sudden spark of pleasure escapes from under my fingers, makes my legs tighten. I can't hold back a throaty *mmmmm.* Bear's breathing grows ragged in my ear. In the background, there's a wet slapping sound.

"Daddy? Are you—"

"Yes," he growls. "Got your picture in front of me. Wish you were here on your knees so I could paint those gorgeous tits."

"Fuck," I gasp.

"Bad girl. Such a bad girl, touching yourself in the dressing room."

Dressing room? I forgot I was even on Earth.

"You gonna punish me?"

"Pinch your nipples," he orders. "Pinch them hard. I want them puffy and sore so I can kiss them better."

I tug my poor pink nubs. The sensation shoots straight to my pussy, liquid gold, pure pleasure.

"Daddy," I gasp.

"You close?"

I slip my hand behind the lace and find the perfect spot. "I'm there."

"Look at the mirror."

I'm so used to obeying his commands, my gaze snaps to my reflection. A wanton redhead sits with her knees spread wide. Her breasts quiver in makeshift bondage, pushed up and on display. Her face and chest are flushed, her pupils dilated, her mouth lush and ready to be kissed.

"Look at that beautiful, perfect goddess. See what I see."

I don't see cellulite. I don't see blemishes or target areas of flab. I don't see my soft belly or dimpled thighs or double chin or jiggly arms. I see a vision of a woman on the cusp of climax, glowing and ready to come on command. Goddess is right. Wanton sex goddess.

"Mine," Bear growls. "All mine."

With a stifled cry, I shudder in climax, mouth open, looking deep into my own eyes. My lashes flutter and I watch my mirror image's chest heave, breasts impossibly large and lovely with peaked nipples and pretty areolas. Her hair's out of control, temples damp from the steamy air. If she were real, I'd kiss her. Two mes, making out? That'd blow Bear and Sawyer's mind.

My mirror image sits back with a smug, satisfied smile on her pouty lips. "Wow," she laughs.

"Yeah," Bear agrees. "You good, baby?"

"Better than good." Fuck this dressing room. If the clothes don't fit, it's their fault, not mine. I point my toes, toss my hair and arch my back, posing with legs and chest on display. I look pretty good, if I say so myself.

"Dressing room therapy. We do it often enough, when you go shopping, you'll think of me."

Pretty effective therapy. I blow a kiss to myself in the mirror. "Thank you, daddy."

"That's my girl."

THE NEXT DAY, I'm back at work, tapping a pen against paper, trying to keep from writing "Evie heart Bear & Sawyer 4 evah" over and over. What is it about orgasms that turn me into a starry-eyed school girl? It's killing my aloof movie star mojo.

"How are you coming on the quarterlies?" My coworker and cubicle neighbor pops his unwanted head in. I smile at my blank computer screen. I know this trick. Ben asks first thing about a project I've never heard of. Once I'm flustered, he dumps some of his own work on me.

Not today. I swirl my chair his direction, poised and ready. "Not my assignment."

At the sight of me Ben's eyes widen, and I smile further. Usually I wear bulky blouses and shapeless skirts, or slacks designed to hide my body. Not today. A dress arrived at my house last night, a red and white polka dot number in a vintage style, along with strappy white espadrilles and a note: *Live a little.* Sawyer getting in on the game of daddy dress up.

"Evie, you look..." Ben blinks at me, or more accurately, at my breasts. "Good. Real good."

"Thank you, Ben," I purr. I look better than good. The dress has a high neck, showing off my shape instead of baring acres of cleavage. It makes me feel modest, but the way it molds to the sharp silhouette of my waist and chest is anything but.

I gloat a moment more. "I don't have time for any of your accounts today. Johnson has me on a bigger project."

Ben nods, a glazed look on his face and I feel triumph. This dress is a weapon, and Ben is my first vanquished foe.

"I need you to forward me the Anderson file." I spin back to face my computer before he can answer, and clack on the keypad. His footsteps humbly retreat. A minute later, his email pops up with an attachment. Victory is mine.

Smirking, I straighten my skirt, shifting a little to get comfortable. The dress and shoes weren't the only gifts. A discreet black box held a bright pink device shaped like a tadpole with a curved tail. When I slip it into my panties (leopard print, Bear-approved) the device presses against my clit and... my butthole. A little weird, but I can play another kinky game. I have two gorgeous men competing to get me off. It's a modern-day sexual adventure: no feelings, no strings attached. I am a suave, sophisticated sex goddess.

I reach for a water bottle and the vibrator in my panties comes to life. I flail, and spill water all over my keyboard.

"Fuck," I hiss, grabbing my cardigan to swab the spillage.

"Everything okay here?" My boss's voice brings me back to reality.

"Yes, fine, Mr. Johnson." I flush.

His eyes dip down to my chest, hugged tight by the polka dots. By the time they make the trip back up, he's flushed too.

"I'm working on the Anderson file." My voice is unnaturally high and loud. Can he hear the buzzing?

"Right. Good." Thankfully, he moves away. Glassy-eyed, I stare at my computer, every once and a while moving the mouse. The vibrator hums merrily along. Just when I've gotten used to it, it stops. I wilt against my desk, mopping my brow with the cardigan. How did they get my exact measurements?

The vibrator stops for a time and I type frantically. A buzz against my sweet spot and I clutch my keyboard, clenching my teeth against overwhelming arousal.

"Evie?" Ben pops in again.

"Yes!" I shout, a little wild.

"You have a delivery." My coworker backs away slowly and a messenger appears.

"Lunch order." The messenger holds up a bag. In it, a sub sandwich and a note. *Take a break to eat.*

How did this happen? I swear off men forever and end up in a sexy game, guided by texts and calls and little notes. I have not one, but two daddies.

I wait until the coast is clear and use a wad of tissues to extricate my vibrating distraction. I drop it into the basket. They'll never know.

I'm halfway through my sandwich, entertaining another check in from Mr. Johnson when my trashcan starts to shake.

"What is that?" My boss peers down just as the vibrator stops. "Did you hear that noise?"

"What noise?" I ask weakly, resisting the urge to grab the trashcan and sprint for the exit.

He's about to walk away when the vibrator starts again.

"That noise."

No, no, no.

"It's coming from—" his head swings towards my trashcan.

"I'm on my period," I blurt.

He looks at me in horror, the trashcan rattling at his feet.

"It's um, a device to help with, um—" Shit, what's the word... "Cramps!" I shout in triumph.

Mr. Johnson's mouth opens and closes like a fish.

"But it didn't work," I explain, hoping he leaves before my blush moves from my chest and unfurls over my entire body. "So I," I motion to the trashcan. Mr. Johnson steps back and almost stumbles. "I just forgot to take out the batteries."

"Ah, yes, yes, of course," my boss stammers and hurries away, looking a little green.

"Sorry!" I call after him and slump over my desk. Now I will have to take a lunch break, to smuggle this demon thing to my car.

My phone comes alive with the "Darth Vader" theme and I fumble for it. Not that I think Mr. Johnson will dare come back and lecture me on personal cellphone use today.

"Evangeline!" My aunt Jen trills as if she's not calling to ask another favor. I should've botched up the last few tasks she and my cousin delegated to me, ensuring I never hear from them again. "Did you order the t-shirts?"

"Yes, Auntie Jen." Six bridesmaid shirts in sizes small, medium, and extra small.

"Oh, and Gwen said she saw you this morning at the Bean Counter. Wearing a dress! Polka dots no less."

"Yep." I don't ask what her friend Gwen was doing spying on me. Gossip is Auntie Jen's full-time job.

"Well, it's nice that you found a shop that caters to big girls. Just make sure you wear black to the wedding."

I grit my teeth.

"Oh, one more thing. Gwen's son's divorce just went through. He needs a date for the wedding, so if you don't have a plus one... his body odor is much better now that he's gotten on medication. Pretty soon he might be able to hold down a job."

"Awww, thanks for thinking of me, but I already have a date." I'll rent one if I have to. Or ask Bear or Sawyer. As soon as I think it, I banish it. This is all for fun. They won't want to be saddled with traditional boyfriend duties, and if I ask, and they refuse, I might not be able to weather the rejection.

At my feet, my trashcan shakes in sad agreement.

CHAPTER 6

ROUND 3

"YOU'RE MEAN." I stomp into Bear's shop. It's after hours, and no one's here. The place smells like gas and motor oil, but all the tools are put away, the counters clean.

"Am I?" He leads me into his office and heads to a fancy Coke machine in the corner. He gets a soda and brings it to me. "How so?"

I hold up the pink thing I exorcised from my trashcan. "I was at work."

"I told you to take a lunch break."

"You're torturing me."

He doesn't quite smile. We both know I love it.

I'm wearing yet another gift, a navy dress with a red cherry pattern. Held up by spaghetti straps, the tight bodice shows some spectacular cleavage. Normally I wouldn't feel comfortable baring so much, but I love showing off for Bear.

I turn in a circle to give him a chance to admire the full view.

His office is open to a sort of showroom. A vintage convertible is on display. Sleek and low to the ground. Lipstick red. I could do my makeup in the gleaming chrome. The rest of the room is a bachelor's dream, full of all sorts of games, including a Ms. Pacman arcade machine.

"You have an air hockey table. And a pool table," I gasp, delighted. If my mechanic had a waiting room like this, I'd be better about getting my car's oil changed. "This place is awesome."

"You want to play?"

"I don't know. I'm pretty competitive." I lean over the mini rink, giving him a heart-stopping view of my breasts. "I'll do anything to win."

"What do I get if I let you?"

"Whatever you want." I saunter over to the pool table. "So how does this work?" I chalk the end of a cue.

"Bend over and I'll show you."

I obey. "Like this?"

"Just like that." He runs a hand up my back before he covers me with his body and guides me into position. "And then you just..." The cue strokes forward. The cue ball hits the red ball with a delicious snick. The three rolls right into the pocket.

"We did it. What's my reward?"

His hands slide up my legs, grip my panties. The next thing I know, his arms flex around me and my ruined thong flutters to the floor.

"Holy fuck," I gasp. He just ripped my underwear off.

His big hand cups my ass under the dress. "What did I tell you about swearing?" he asks, just as his palm connects with my right butt cheek, hard.

"I thought you were joking!"

"I should put you over my knee," he growls, and smacks my butt again. At the sting, arousal spikes through me. My legs give out. I collapse on the pool table, panting.

"You know the rules."

I nod.

"Say, 'Yes, daddy,'" he commands.

"Yes, daddy," I repeat, and his right hand comes between my legs rewarding me with the most delicious touch. His left arm snakes around my waist, holding me in place. I let my head rest on his chest, intent on the movement of his fingers. He strokes me to the edge and then withdraws.

"Not fair!" I cry as he pulls away. My pussy throbs.

"Later," he says, and hugs me to him as he pulls out his cellphone and calmly orders a pizza. I'm not hungry for anything but Bear. You'd think I'd be used to him playing the long game. I caress his jean-clad crotch and he catches my wrist, shaking his head a little.

I pout at him until he hangs up. "You ripped my underwear."

"I'll buy you a new pair."

"Daddy Morebucks."

His chuckle is an earthquake under my cheek. I wriggle upwards and find his mouth and then we're kissing, lips pulling and persuading, a climax-of-the-movie kiss. After a moment, he stands, taking me with him. My legs wrap around him as he strides to the vintage Cadillac. He lays me back and my hair spills out of my updo, auburn splashing across the red paint. One of Bear's big hands grips my calf, hitching it higher. I'm open and angled to fit his body between my legs.

"Wait—what about the pizza?"

"What about it?" He pulls me close and presses forward.

The Cadillac is the right height for him to take me. All he has to do is unzip his jeans and free himself. "Sawyer said you like a little exhibitionism."

A laugh stutters out of me. His hips roll against me, stealing my thoughts and my breaths, one by one. I hook a leg around his waist and grind against him, not caring that I'll leave a wet spot on his jeans.

"Please." I brace against the car hood, straining towards him.

Bear slips a hand under my bottom. "You want this?"

"Yes, yes, yes." In a moment of inspiration, I unzip the bodice and strip the spaghetti straps down. The top was too tight to wear a bra. My breasts spill out and I arch my back, presenting them to his touch.

"Fu—" he almost swears.

"Fuck me, Daddy," I breathe.

He pulls a condom out of his pocket before he shucks down his jeans and tugs me against him. I watch, panting, as he sheaths his cock. He finds my entrance and presses slowly forward, easing in as my legs tremble and my body stretches around him.

He's not smiling, but he's beautiful. I lay a hand against his taut jaw, then slide it to the back of his neck to hold on.

Each thrust is its own punishment and reward. I dig my nails into giant flexing muscles and let my orgasm rise.

"I... I can't... I'm gonna..."

"Come, baby," he says, and I shake apart.

"Omigod, omigod..."

Bear slams into me, one hand braced by my head, the other holding my leg. My first climax rolls through me and washes back into a second. And still he fucks me. He is immortal, he's a god. This will never end.

My ears ring with my cries, I grip Bear so hard I'm sure

I've drawn blood. Catching my breath between climaxes, I surge upwards and bite his neck.

Bear's body jerks. His hips snap into me a final time, grinding down as he finds his release. I surrender, my body melting into his, accepting the final plundering thrust, showering him with kisses and cooing adoration. His lips find mine, but he lets me lead, sweet and quiet worship.

Satisfied, I lean back. For once, his record cool is shattered. His eyes are open, vulnerable, searching my face.

I lick my lips. "Thank you, daddy." I try for Marilyn Monroe levels of coy, but my voice cracks a little.

It was supposed to be a game, a fling. The most important rule: "don't get attached." Grab your orgasm and run.

This is not just sex. How can we just walk away from this?

"I guess I can orgasm with a guy." I let my arms fall away and lean back to tug up my dress. Pulling away, even as we're still connected. He's still inside me.

"Evie, I..."

I press a finger to his lips. He can't speak and break the spell. As it is, I'm not sure if I'm going to leave with my heart intact.

"Listen—" he starts when the shop buzzer makes me lurch against him.

"Pizza delivery!"

"Leave it on the stoop," Bear shouts, and I burst out laughing.

BEAR'S OFFICE HAS A COUCH. After cleaning me up, he carries me there and feeds me pizza. A girl could get used to this.

You will not get used to this, I scold. *You love 'em and leave 'em now, remember?*

The big screen in the game room has a movie silently playing. Grace Kelly and Cary Grant riding in a blue convertible. *Poise, elegance.* I try not to slurp cheese off my last slice. I do need the calories. Bear strokes my calf absently.

"When is the wedding?"

"What?" I squawk. "Oh, yes. My cousin's wedding. It's, uh, in two weeks."

I wait for him to say more but he does not. I finish my meal and crawl up on his lap. He hasn't said much since our mutual Cum-aggedon. I know he felt it like I did. In my experience, guys tend to ignore those feelings. They date me for a bit until my weirdness starts to grate, then they leave me for someone thinner. *If she'd stick to a diet, maybe she could keep a man.* My Auntie Jen has one solution. I have another: don't try to keep one.

"This was fun," I sigh.

A smile ghosts over Bear's mouth. "I meant for us to end up in bed."

"It's okay," I murmur, stroking his short hair. "We have plenty of time." I say it before I remember it's not true.

Bear goes quiet for a while, gripping my hips with a troubled look on his face.

"What's wrong?" I ask.

"Why do I get the feeling you have one foot out the door?"

"Because after a few more nights together, the competition's over. Don't be sad." I settle into his lap, cuddling as he strokes me in thoughtful silence.

"Spend the night with me," he whispers.

"Tonight?"

"Come see the hot tub."

"I still don't have a bathing suit."

"Do you need one?"

Oh my.

"GLASS OF WINE?" Bear calls, heading to his kitchen.

"Sounds good." I sashay slowly behind him. Am I really doing this? I take a deep breath and accept the wine. Liquid courage.

"Drink that, and I'll get the tub goin'."

Geez. I take a gulp of Chardonnay. There's not enough liquid in the world to give me courage to bare my body in front of my dream man.

"Are we really doing this?" I wrinkle my nose. "Skinny dipping?"

He chuckles softly. "Bedroom. I have a surprise for you."

"Another vibrator?" I raise a brow.

"You'll see." He ushers me on with a hand on my back, switching on the light to his bedroom and guiding me to the bed. He's already hard, his ready erection brushing my back. I'm about to grind my ass on him and get this party started when I notice the open box on the bed. Inside are a few baby blue pieces of fat string. I gulp.

A bikini. Right up there with a dressing room mirror as my nemesis.

Bear's heat hits my back as he wraps huge arms around me. "You can wear this or nothing."

"Door number three?"

"Third option is you wear what I choose... but with a red ass."

"I'll try the bikini."

He kisses my neck and leaves me to it. I approach the bed like it holds a snake about to bite. With two fingers I pick up the miniscule bathing suit and bare my teeth. I have shoe laces thicker than the stringy bottoms. And the top, I only hope the two triangles are enough to tame my ample breasts. Otherwise, the neighbors will get a show.

A knock on the door. "Evie? Need help?"

"No, I got it! One sec." I rush to slip into the two pieces, tying and fastening, shifting the pieces of fabric to contain my curves. The bikini does a token job of hiding my naughty bits, displaying more than it shelters. My lingerie covers more skin.

I stride out of the bedroom before I lose my nerve. "Bear?"

"Out here," he calls from the back deck. I head through his back room and brush a stack of towels on the washing machine. Grabbing one, I wind it around me. Good thing these towels are large, big as a sheet. I traipse out in my makeshift toga, carrying another towel for Bear. He's already in the hot tub, but maybe I can distract him while I whip away my towel and slip under the water like a magician doing a trick. I could shake the extra towel like a matador, but he's Bear, not Bull. There has to be a way to execute this maneuver—

"Evie," Bear calls and I realize I've been standing beside the hot tub, lost in thought.

"Yes?"

"Baby," he's smiling. "Lose the towel."

I set his down and hold the one around me higher as I step into the water. I try to think of a moviestar to model, but my mind is blank.

The towel snags on something and I yelp, clutching it tighter. I look around but the something the towel snagged on is Bear's hand. He gives a tug and I toss the towel away, sitting real fast. There. I slip under the water, relaxing as the ripples hide my dimpled thighs. Having saved my towel, Bear turns to me with a wide, shark's grin. He starts for me and I press back into a corner.

"I love the water," I blurt to distract him. "Auntie Jen took me and my cousin to the pool every summer."

It works. He takes a seat and leans back.

"For years, all the way through middle school. Of course, when I turned thirteen, she made me wear a t-shirt over my bathing suit. I was well-endowed, even then."

He's listening, but he reaches down and seizes my ankle, pulling my foot into his lap where he can knead it.

"It was weird to have breasts that young. Grown men hit on me."

His strong fingers rub my calf.

"They were shocked when I told them how young I was. I had the body of a woman, I wanted to be girl."

"And now?" His hands work past my knee, massaging my entire leg.

"I still want to be thin. I have an hourglass figure with a ton of sand. A fudge ton. Literally, created by fudge."

Bear's lips purse.

"Tell me you don't like thin women," I challenge before he can correct me.

"I like thin women," he shrugs.

I stiffen.

"But I love this." He's gotten closer, his hands caressing my sides under the water, eyes on my breasts. "Baby, if you can look like this—"

"I have a belly," I pout.

He frowns, eyebrows drawing together as he reluctantly drops his gaze below my nipples. "Oh look, you do." His big hand slides over my pooch, completely covering it. He can hold my whole dang belly chub in the palm of one hand. "It's so cute."

Cute? Cute?! Years of agonized mirror time, eating chalky protein bars in place of meals, wearing t-shirts over my tankini to cover my body—and he says, 'Cute?'

My head explodes.

"What's wrong?" he asks. He must have noticed the smoking hole where my head used to be.

"Cute..." I choke out.

"Yeah," his thumb strokes up and down, and all the blood my head doesn't need rushes to my fun zone. "And soft. So soft," his head dips, his hair brushing the tops of my sensitized breasts as he nuzzles between them. "And sweet." His hand dips into the triangle of fabric covering my pussy. His fingers hit their target. A minute later, the rest of me explodes.

Bear watches me writhe, a lazy happiness crinkling his eyes. "I take it back," he says. His thumb at my nipple, stroking, stroking. "If you lose an ounce, I'll take a belt to your ass."

With effort, I pull my brain back together. "Is that really a threat?"

"Yeah." He grips my hips and pulls me onto his lap, and I forget how to talk again. I forget everything and let him pull me under. I don't surface until we're back in bed, my wet hair spread onto towel covering the pillow, the rest of me wrapped in Bear. I don't even protest when Bear whispers, "Oh, and Evie? Sawyer says pack the suit for his turn with you."

~

ROUND 4

"You're quiet." Sawyer grabs a bag of gear out of the back of his Jeep, and catches my hand, pulling me towards the beach.

"I'm wearing a bikini. In public."

"You look great." His smile dazzles. I hold his hand and keep my cover up closed with the other.

Sawyer leads me down the dunes to an empty stretch of sand. Two cliffs rise on either side of the beach like sentinels. There's no one here but birds.

"What is this place?"

"The wildlife sanctuary. Don't worry, I got permission." He pauses to dig out a camera from his bag and sling it over his shoulder.

"What are you doing?" I ask a bit nervously.

"I'm doing a photography session with a model."

"Okay. Who's the model?"

Sawyer just looks at me.

"Oh no. Come on."

He fights a smile.

"Awww," I whine. "Do I have to?"

He advances, grinning. His teeth are shark white. When he gets close, he tugs me forward by my hips, bringing me the rest of the way. It never fails to get me hot, the way he and Bear manhandle me.

"I want you to know how beautiful you are."

My blush spreads like a red tide over my exposed skin. So, basically, my entire body, all but a few inches.

"Say, '*yes, daddy.*'"

Those are the magic words. I tingle just reciting them—

Bear has me primed for a reward with those magic words. "Yes, daddy."

Still smiling, he draws me to a few rocks and has me sit. I get to keep my gauzy cover up, for now. Not that the see-through fabric is doing much to camouflage my body. He tugs my hair tie out and my hair tumbles around my face.

"There," he breathes. "Just like that. Don't move."

"Or else?"

"I'll tie you up." I wait for him to grin, but he's perfectly serious. He backs away and starts setting up equipment. I bite my lip and look out at the ocean.

"That's it, Evie. Just relax."

I flinch at the sound of the shutter.

"Wait." He strides forward, catches my chin and kisses the hell out of me. His lips leave mine for a moment; I make a sound like "nuuuh."

"Much better," he says. I barely note when he backs away and starts taking pictures.

The sun beats down, bathing our fearless heroine in radiant light. Her red hair shimmers. She moves, and it spills across her glorious chest. Click goes the camera shutter.

I am a model. I am an object of beauty with creamy skin and auburn locks, wearing nothing but a translucent robe and a few pieces of fat string. I am ephemeral.

Slowly, I strip off my coverall. I'm the star in my own movie, crossing the beach, staring at the horizon. Click goes the camera shutter. I shield my eyes a moment. Click, click, click. Then I head towards the surf, a sea goddess, a mermaid returning home.

The ocean surges to greet me, covering my feet with green froth and pieces of seaweed.

"Ygghah!!" I gasp, staggering back. The water is absolutely freezing.

"Yeah, it's cold." Sawyer laughs like a crazy man.

"How do you surf in this?"

He shrugs. "Wetsuits. Keep going. What were you going to do?"

"I was going to get in the water, but it's too cold." My mermaid dreams are dashed.

"Sometimes you gotta suffer for art."

"Is that what this is? Art?" I mutter, but I do my best. I dance in the surf until my toes are numb. I retreat to dry land until the sun bakes me. My sunscreen is long gone. Sawyer moves around me, capturing moments with each decisive click. He's in the zone, totally focused.

I decide to seduce him.

"Mmmm," I murmur, sliding my hands down my lush body. My breasts really are a work of art. I could just tug this string and they'd be free...

I wait a moment for Sawyer to stop and ask what I'm doing. When he doesn't, I continue. I'm topless, lounging in the surf. I roll in the sand. I tousle my hair and look over my shoulder, coy. I stretch like a cat in the sun.

"Yes," Sawyer murmurs, hot and husky like I'm pleasuring him. "That's it, baby. Keep going."

I grow hot enough to return to the water. I lie half in, half out of the surf, letting the water rush over me. My nipples are hard enough to cut glass.

My cheeks are hot. I've gone pink like undercooked meat. Another hour and I'll be a lobster. Not to mention the sand up in my crotch, turning my bikini bottoms into sandpaper. My hair's stringing, I'm sweaty and... gah, how do bikini models do it?

"Uncomfortable?" Sawyer asks, and when I grumble yes, he nods to my bikini bottoms. "Take it off."

"What?"

"Take them off."

"But—"

"Do you trust me?"

I bite my lip and nod.

He crouches close, "I won't let anything bad happen to you. Okay?"

"Okay," I whisper.

I end up on my knees in the surf, waving the white cover up over my head like a flag. *I surrender.*

"That's a wrap, baby." Sawyer puts his camera away.

And then he meets me in the surf, grabbing my wet, sandy, sweaty body and hauling me against him. He's rock-hard and ready. He got this hard just watching me...

I make a noise like "rauwrrr" and pounce. We're rolling in the sand, attacking each other with our mouths. I slide against him, ignoring the sandpaper grit.

"Here," he dips us in the ocean, ignoring my yelp. Once we're clean of sand, he carries me up, shivering, to a rock spread with our towel. He sits, frees himself and drives up into me so hard I cry out.

"My beautiful girl," he murmurs, holding my hips and surging. I rock on top of him.

"You gotta ask permission," he reminds me, and my body clenches on him so hard he bucks.

"Fuck, Evie, come."

I throw back my head and ride the waves of pleasure.

A seagull flies in lazy circles over us as Sawyer carries me to the car and sets me, wrapped in nothing but the towel, in the seat. My wet hair splays over the leather. I'm a mermaid come to land in the arms of her prince.

"That was great," I murmur when Sawyer returns from putting up his equipment. His jaw jerks up in agreement. "I bet I'm not like most models you use."

"No," he agrees. "You're not."

Ouch. I blink at my window. It's just a game. I can do this.

"It sure is fun waiting to see what you guys can come up with next. I'm looking forward to the next round with you."

"Right."

His clipped tone makes me tense. I spend the next few minutes trying out a few questions and responses in my head. Finally, I settle on, "Are you and Bear... okay with all this?"

"Sure." He shrugs and gives me a Hollywood smile. He doesn't meet my eyes. "It's just a game, Evie. You have nothing to lose."

He's wrong. I do have something to lose. My heart.

~

"HEY, bitch. How's the meat sandwich?"

"Mina..."

"Oh, that's right," she laughs, "You're the meat in the middle of the sandwich. Lucky bitch."

"Stop."

"Am I making you blush? Take a picture and send it to me. Your blushes are epic."

"Gee, thanks. No, I will not send a picture." This reminds me too much of Bear's panty rule. I cover a cheek with my palm, and yes, my skin is hot to the touch.

"Well? The dates?" she prompts when I don't answer.

"They're not dates."

"The fuck buddy stuff, then."

Fuck buddy. That's exactly the word for me. "Carp," I mutter.

"Carp?" Mina asks.

"I'm trying to swear less."

"Fuck that!"

"Mina... I have a question." As soon as I say it, I regret it, but Mina will never let up until I ask. "Do these guys date? Long relationships?"

"No, not really. I asked my brothers and they don't know of any girl that's lasted more than a few months. But that doesn't mean they wouldn't change their mind. You know, for you."

"Yeah, right."

"What are you doing with them?"

"Nothing. Just a stupid bet." I'm nothing to them. I mean, they're both bedding me. What guy is okay with that? They probably think I'm a slut. An easy lay. Even if I did want to date one of them, at this point I'd be sloppy seconds. "They're just foolin' around. It means nothing." Except for Bear's little project to rehabilitate my self-esteem. Maybe he thinks he's doing me a favor, fixing me to go on after the competition is over. Sawyer and him competing to spoil me, make me feel special.

When I think about it all ending, I don't feel special. I feel like a used soccer ball.

I realize Mina is talking.

"Why do you do this to yourself? Don't you think they'd be interested in you?"

"Look at me. Look at the girls they're usually with."

"Fuck that. You. Are. Gorgeous. I don't know how many times I've told you. You're like a short Christina Hendricks. Total bombshell."

I say nothing and she mutters, "Your fucking aunt..."

"Hey, remember my cousin Genevieve?" I change the subject. "She's getting married."

"Awesome. Which guy are you taking to the wedding?"

I sigh. "Neither."

"You should make them arm wrestle for the privilege. My money's on Bear, although Sawyer has a good shot. He's not as big, but he's sneaky. Has he tried coming in your backdoor?"

"Goodbye, Mina."

I'm rushing around to get ready for work. I go to grab underwear out of my special "Bear-bought" lingerie drawer and come up with a big fat handful of nothing. Crap. All these orgasms and living my best sex life now, and I've completely forgotten the mundane details that used to swamp me.

I missed laundry day. Which means no underwear. I grimace at my phone. I have to tell Bear.

I procrastinate. By the time I get to my phone, his text is waiting. *Baby, you forgetting something?*

Eep! I'm all sweaty-palmed, not to mention bare-assed beneath my fitted skirt.

I dial Bear standing by the door. Maybe I can explain better over the phone. "The thing is," I launch in as soon as he greets me. "I didn't do laundry. So. Um. I'm out of underwear."

Silence.

"That's why I didn't ask you. I was going to go... without."

I fidget with my blouse, tucking it in and leaving it unbuttoned to reveal a silky cami underneath. With a tight black skirt and my hair up in a bun, I've made a decent attempt at 'sexy librarian'.

"So, you're goin' to work... without underwear?"

"Yeah. But I look real cute!" I snap a picture and text it really quick. The phone angle gives a spectacular shot of my boobs and cocked hip. The cami shimmers. The stretchy skirt makes sweet love to my curvy butt.

More silence, but he's breathing a teensy, tiny bit heavier. Finally, he says, "Consequences, baby."

Shiver.

Consequences. I tap a pencil against my teeth. What does Bear mean? I have to admit I'm curious.

I never expected a game like this.

"Special delivery, Evie." Ben marches into my cubicle. I whirl and give him a "your book is overdue" glare and he halts in the entrance.

"Thank you, Benjamin," I murmur and spin back to my computer. "You may leave it on the counter."

He obeys and lingers, probably hoping I'll open it in front of him. Fat chance.

"Did you finish the report summary Mr. Lui's wanted?" I toss Ben a curveball. See how he likes it.

"Uh—"

"Be a dear and forward it to me by three? Thank you so much."

He retreats and I smile at my gift. Evie 1, Ben 0.

I make myself wait a full ten minutes before swiveling to study the lovely gift-wrapping. There's a note on top: "Open in private."

I hustle to the bathroom and rip open my gift, nearly

flinging a sexy scrap of lace across the room. Fifteen panties folded into bright rows like candy.

My thighs clench and I fumble for my phone.

I text Bear. *Daddy, will you pick which color?*

Pink.

With shaking hands, I draw my new panties on and send him a picture.

Good girl.

I seriously consider rubbing one out in the bathroom. By the time I get home, I'm floating. Not even a phone call from my aunt, demanding I finalize the flower arrangements, can bring me down. I catch sight of myself in the mirror as I'm shimmying out of my work clothes, and can't resist stroking myself over the silky lace, the color of new rosebuds. I'm so keyed up, and I'm already in trouble, so I might as well enjoy it.

My phone rings just as my finger slips off my clit, detonating the orgasm I've been dying for all day.

"Hello?" I answer, breathless.

"Evie," Bear drawls my name. He knows.

"Sorry, daddy," I come clean right away. "I, um, touched myself. I came."

"Consequences, baby." A smug smile lurks in his voice. I squirm, ready to come again.

"What are you going to do?"

"Teach my baby to obey."

When Bear opens the door to his place, my stomach flip-flops at the sight of him. Tonight wasn't planned. I'm outside the boundaries of the game.

"I packed a bag." I shrug said bag off my shoulder.

“Good baby.” He takes it and guides me straight into the bedroom. I stop in my tracks at the sight of the items he’s prepped and laid out on a towel at the end of the bed. Bear sets my bag down, takes a seat and crooks a finger at me.

“What, no foreplay?” I ask, my voice as light as I can make it even as I shiver in his arms. He pulls me between his legs, running his hands up and down my arms, squeezing reassuringly.

“This is punishment,” he says simply. I stare at the implements lined up on the towel: a crop, a cane, a hairbrush and small black bulb-shaped thing—a butt plug.

“Do I need, like, a safeword?”

“If you want. If you say ‘stop’, I’ll stop.” He angles his head. “Do you want to stop?”

Tempting, but no. I shake my head, which pleases him. He’s still massaging me, moving from my arms to my back and hips.

“I’m nervous,” I tell him.

“The only thing you need to do tonight is obey me. If it gets too much, tell me to stop.”

“Right.”

He turns me to lean against him, half sitting in his lap. His arms lock around me, his right hand sliding into my yoga pants and panties to delve into my soft, wet folds.

“Wet for me.”

Major understatement.

He strokes until my hips are writhing and clamps me tighter. “Be good, baby.”

“Daddy... please... I’m close.”

He pulls his fingers from my panties. I groan but suck his digits clean when he presents them to me, one by one.

He pulls off my top and pushes my bra down under my breasts to push them up. He spends some time teasing the sensitive mounds until I'm grinding in his lap, so keyed up I could orgasm from a few nipple tugs. Which is amazing, considering how hard it used to be for me to orgasm.

"Daddy—"

He stops and nuzzles my neck. "Obey. Do you want to please me?" He lifts the hair off my shoulder to collar me with kisses.

"Yes, yes, yes." More than anything.

"Obey me."

"It's hard," I whine, and grind down on his dick. *Yep, super hard.*

"You're being so good." Now his hand is back in my pants, cupping me like he owns me. Which he does.

"Yes, daddy. Please—"

He brings me right to the edge and stops, flipping me off his lap and onto the bed. He looms over me, gathering my wrists over my head. My heart leaps at the stern look in his eye.

"Whose pussy is this?" Rough fingers skewer me, twisting sharply. It'd hurt but I'm sopping wet.

"Yours."

"And who do your orgasms belong to." Another finger and I moan.

"You, daddy."

"That's right. Mine." He pulls the fingers out and wipes them on my yoga pants. "Up," he barks. "Over my lap. Take your punishment like a good girl, and I might let you come."

I crawl over his broad lap. His thighs are rock hard, his profile solemn and unyielding above me. This disciplinarian Bear is unlike anything I've ever seen. I love it so much.

"Start with a spanking. Then you get the brush. Finish you off with a taste of something stronger. Squirm too much, things will escalate. Understand?"

"Yes, daddy."

It's only a game. But it feels so real.

His big hand squeezes my bottom before the spanking commences. I let my head hang down. Draped over his lap, accepting each swat on my ass, my mind goes to a zen-like place. The sting, muffled by the spandex of my yoga pants, centers me.

Halfway through, he pulls down my pants. The first smack makes me jerk. No more Mr. Nice Palm. My bottom is already warm, though, so the new intensity plateaus.

My ass is hot before he stops.

"Good, baby. Now the brush."

Fuck.

"What was that?"

Oops, I said it out loud. "Sorry, daddy."

"You will be."

The dark promise makes my pussy clench. The hard, wooden surface crashes onto my warm buttocks, lighting up my nerve endings and making me jerk.

I yelp, but Bear's noticed my added wetness.

"You like this?" He stops and rubs my clit. I spasm for an entirely different reason.

"Oh my God."

"You can call me 'daddy.'"

I smile to myself, enjoying the attention to my naughty bits. He alternates rubbing with smacks. How am I not supposed to come from this?

"Four more with the brush." He taps my left buttock before the wood slaps down. I whimper and wait. Right, left, right. And done. Now his fingers frig me harder.

"You gonna come?"

"Yes," I wail, and he stops. My orgasm dissipates.

"Not yet," he says, not unsympathetically. "You have a choice. One with the cane or three with the crop."

"Then I can come?"

"Greedy baby. Yes. If you wear the buttplug, you can come."

Unfffff. I squirm a little to hide my excitement.

"Need an answer, Evie."

"Cane." My voice is small. I hear it hurts like a mother.

"You sure?"

"Yes, daddy." I'm curious about the crop too. Later, I'll ask him for a taste.

"Cane it is." But he takes his sweet time, stirring up my orgasm, pausing, letting it die. I'm all worked up and red-faced by the time he lays the hard, thin implement against my upper thighs. With a whoosh, it whips down.

Arghasdfasdf. The cane paints a line of fire across my legs. I'll feel that tomorrow.

"Now the plug," Bear says.

Oh, sweet Jesus in a hammock. I grit my teeth through the indignity of him lubing up my back hole.

"Gonna claim you here."

I grunt.

Now, with the plug in my bottom and clit throbbing from the intermittent attention, I feel like a corked champagne bottle, shaken and about to explode.

Bear draws things out, too, rubbing up and down my legs and back, squeezing my poor ass cheeks and playing with the plug until I moan.

"Are you going to touch without permission?" His fingers sink into my sopping pussy. My climax builds, tightening my hips.

"No, daddy."

"Are you going to ask me what to wear every morning?"

"Yes, daddy. Please—"

"Come—"

I buck on his lap. His fingers thrust deep, extending the shockwaves of pleasure spiraling out from my lower back. Vaguely aware of the juices running over his hand, I grab his leg to steady myself.

"That's right. Let daddy take care of you."

"Thank you, daddy," I say as soon as I catch my breath.

"You're welcome, baby. The thought of you going to work, sans panties." He growls something that might be a swear word, except he doesn't swear. "Feel what you do to me."

I drop to my knees and nearly rip his pants in my haste to get him out. "Is this for me?"

"Yes. You earned it; you take care of it."

With a grin, I do just that.

When I leave the next day, trying not to think about how waking up next to Bear feels right, there's a text waiting for me from Sawyer. An address.

What's this?

Tonight at 7. Be there. Is all I get. Bear's rubbing off on Sawyer.

The destination turns out to be an industrial area of town. Sawyer opens the door to a shady looking warehouse.

"Everything all right?"

"It is now." He tucks a stand of hair behind my ear, cups my chin and kisses me deeply before drawing me inside. We pass through a large dark space, a room glowing with a low red light, and climb up to a loft lit by the windows above. It's a sparsely decorated living space, with one of Sawyer's black and white prints, a leather couch that's seen better days, and a big screen TV. Derelict chic. I bite my lip before I can ask if he's squatting here.

Sawyer turns to me and I forget my surroundings.

"So," he says. "Bear told me he got extra time with you."

"Um. Yes." I have the cane mark to prove it.

He gives me a wicked grin that makes my knees wobble. "My turn."

"What are we going to do?"

"Netflix and chill."

That doesn't sound too—

"My way."

Another grin. Another wobble.

"Strip for me."

Um.

"Do you need help?"

Biting my lip, I pull off my shirt and wriggle out of my work slacks.

Sawyer runs his hand down my leg, cups my bottom. "Did Bear approve these?" He plucks the lace of my new thong panties. Cream colored.

I nod.

He hooks his fingers under them and rips through the thin straps. "Mine now."

Holy Hannah, he just ripped off my panties!

"Blue is more your color," I say. "I have a pair you can wear."

He grins. "For that I'll turn your ass pink."

My cheeks flame. Bear's spanked me, but Sawyer hasn't. Does it seem weird? Not weird, different. And exciting.

He seats himself on the tattered leather couch.

"Get my bag."

"Your purse?"

"Man purse. Murse."

"Whatever. Just call it a purse."

"You really want a red ass, don't you?"

"Spank me, daddy." I wink.

He groans. The front of his jeans grows tight.

I pad back with his murse and set it warily beside him. He reaches in and pulls out—rope. Lots and lots of rope.

"Have you ever been tied up?"

I blink at him a little unsure.

"Turn around. Hands on your head." After I obey, hesitatingly, he stands and winds the rope around my chest, stopping to undo my bra before looping the rope over and under my breasts. They stand at attention, begging to be touched but he's frowning, in the zone, kneeling to loop rope around my legs and hips, makeshift rope panties.

"Too tight?" he tugs, and I grunt in the negative. "Don't worry, I've always got a pair of scissors close."

"You don't just rip the ropes off with your bare hands?"

He swats my bottom, lightly.

"Is that all you got?" I sass.

"Bear didn't say you were a brat." He sounds happy.

"Maybe I'm good with Bear."

"He gets good and I get naughty?"

I raise a brow and he chuckles, wrapping me with more rope. "I'm okay with that."

He concentrates on tying a final knot. "There." He tugs and I sway a little. "It's supposed to be snug." He rises and takes me in for the first time. The rope loops around my legs, slides over my crotch before connecting to the winding masterpiece that frames my breasts.

"Evie," he sounds pained, like he's tied up instead of me. I like. "I knew it would look good but..."

His thumbs stroke my nipples. I grab his wrists and he makes a pleased sound.

Next thing I know my wrists are loosely bound behind me. My shoulders aren't drawn back too much, but I can't free my hands. Then he's leading me closer to the couch.

"Now what?"

"Now" he tips me over his lap, guiding me. His hand smacks my ass. "How hard does Bear usually spank you?"

"I don't even know how to answer that. Why don't you ask him to show you? Show don't tell, the best way to find out—ow!"

"I've had about enough of your lip," Sawyer lets loose a flurry of smacks onto my bare ass. The rope frames my cheeks, similar to the weave around my breasts. He tugs the single crotch rope and lightning shoots through my brain.

"Like your rope?"

"Nnghnghh," I grunt and he laughs. He produces a remote from somewhere and clicks on the huge screen. All of a sudden, we're watching a movie, him clothed, me naked, tied up and tipped over his lap.

"Are you gonna free me?" I ask after a few minutes.

"Hush or I'll gag you."

Guess not.

I don't complain again, and he rewards me, fondling my breasts, running strong fingers over my labia where they're plumped around the crotch rope. He makes it vibrate between my legs and tells me I can come. As soon as my orgasm washes through me, he starts building another.

I don't pay much attention to the movie.

He plucks the rope between my legs again and again, and loosens it to play with my ass. Before I know it, his index finger circles my back hole. I tighten my cheeks.

"Uhhhh..."

"You a virgin back here?"

"Yeah."

"I call dibs."

"Bear already did."

"He's not the boss of me." Is that a tinge of bitterness in his tone? I stare at the screen and let the silence stretch. "Sorry," Sawyer mutters after a minute. He mutes the movie and arranges me on my back, head on the cushioned arm. "If you need a break, tell me to stop," he orders, and lowers his bright head between my legs.

Turns out the only thing better than his fingers plucking the crotch string is his tongue. I wriggle and writhe and do everything but tell him to stop. My fingers itch to dig themselves into his hair.

"Sawyer," I finally gasp, and he raises his head.

"Yes?"

"Please fuck me."

"With pleasure."

It's almost midnight before he lets me go. He untied me long ago, only to tie and wind me up again in a different way. I wobble to my clothes and sling them on, not caring that they're inside out. I had awesome Shibari sex with Sawyer. My strut home won't be a Walk of Shame, but a Walk of Triumph.

Sawyer watches me dress, hands in pockets. "Can I get you anything?"

After all those orgasms, I'm probably dehydrated, but there's no kitchen in sight. Not even a mini-fridge.

I wave 'no, thank you' and something flickers in his eyes, a hesitancy I've never seen in him. He's usually so confident. "I'd invite you to spend the night, but—" he shrugs at the bed-less loft.

"It's probably better if we don't."

"You spent the night at Bear's." He's so solemn, all of a sudden, I don't recognize him.

"Yes, well… that was a mistake."

"Really." His voice is flat.

I edge towards the stairs. "You know how this is all temporary."

"Evie—"

"I had a good time," I rush. "Consider yourself even. I won't let my night with Bear skew the competition."

"Fuck the competition," he mutters, running a hand through his blond locks.

"Night," I gulp, and escape, practically running out of the warehouse. I don't even snoop in the weirdly lit room like I wanted too. It's better this way. Safer. Stick to the competition, enjoy the moments, because it's all we're gonna have. In two more rounds, this whole thing is over.

CHAPTER 7

ROUND 5

"WHAT IS THIS PLACE?" We're back in the industrial part of town. I forgot to ask Sawyer when I met him here a few nights ago.

Bear helps me pick my way across some broken concrete to the warehouse door. "This is Sawyer's studio."

"Is he here?" I don't know how Sawyer will like Bear bringing me here. Something tells me their friendship is now a bit strained.

"Not now. Come on. I have something to show you."

Inside is pretty dim, like the first time. I step into a dust-mote filled patch of light.

"What is it you wanted to show me?"

He flicks the lights and they stutter to life. I'm in the middle of a circle of photos, blown up to cover painting sized canvases. My face reflected a dozen times.

"Oh my God." It's me, at the beach, hair blown across my face, curves on full display. It's beautiful.

I'm beautiful.

And I'm crying.

"Thank you," I whisper. "Thank you so much."

"Anything, baby," he murmurs. "Anything for you."

BEAR TAKES me back to his townhouse for drinks and dinner from the grill.

"You play dirty," I tell him. "I should tell Sawyer you have an edge because you feed me."

"Not the reason I do it, babe."

I gesture to the grill and the patio table set for two with my wineglass. "So you're saying this isn't all so you can take the lead?"

He drops a kiss on my forehead before he goes back to turning the chicken. "I like watching you eat."

As usual, his words make me all glowy. I flirt with him through the main course, running my foot up his calf and suggesting he eat something sweet for dessert. I'll get him worked up and then tell him there's no way I can declare a winner in the competition. I'll just have to eat his food and wear the clothes he buys me and ask his permission to come forever.

I'm helping him clean up when my phone rings. Mina. I step into the hall and answer it with a lazy, "Hey."

"Hey, girl." I straighten at the unusual greeting. "You still fooling around with Bear and Sawyer?"

"Why?"

"Is it serious?"

I swallow. "I don't know. What did you find out?" I head to the bathroom and shut the door. "Tell me."

"Sawyer's photography has gotten some interest. He's got a show in a gallery in San Diego, and there's a space for him to be an artist-in-residence."

"What?"

"I was hoping you knew. He's leaving soon."

I clear my throat. "Well, that's good."

"There's more. I did more digging on Bear."

"Don't tell me has an ex-wife or love child," I try to joke.

"Nope, just a profile on Fetlife. He's been looking for a while. But he recently changed his status to "in a relationship."

"Oh," I choke out. "Well, good for him." I can't stop the sinking feeling. I wanted to know whether this was for real or only temporary? I just got proof.

It's just a game, and it's almost over. No matter the outcome, I lose.

Still staring at my phone, I walk back to the living room. A big photo greets me. Another black and white of me laughing in the surf.

It must be a regular game they play: pick up a girl and fix her. I was fine playing along until they made it seem like I meant something to them. But I was just Bear's project. And Sawyer? He took these photos because he needed them for a show.

Maybe he'll let me keep one as a memory of when I was happy.

"There's a game on. Figured we can watch that." He stops when he sees the look on my face.

"Did you know?" I jerk my head toward the picture. "Did you know about Sawyer's show?"

"Yes," he says and frowns. "Did you?"

"No." Suddenly my chest is seizing and there's not enough air in the room. "I need to go." If I don't get out now, I'm going to break down. It'll be like dressing room panic, but a thousand times worse. Cry-maggedon.

"Evie," he comes close and cups my face. "Look at me."

My eyes slide to the left, to the right, anywhere but his.

"I can't," I whisper. "I'm sorry. I can't do this."

I scramble for the door.

"Evie," Bear calls. I scurry to my car, slam the door and lock it. I waste no time putting him in the rearview mirror.

Over the next few hours, my phone bleats repeatedly. Bear calling, then Sawyer. I drive aimlessly.

I do send one text to Sawyer. *Were you going to ask me before using my photos at your photography show?*

I'm not in my apartment ten minutes before there's a knock on the door.

"Go away," I shout.

"Evie, come on." Sawyer. He sounds broken, which only makes me angry. Why should he be broken up over this? It was only a fucking game.

I open the door with the chain in. "Game over. I call a draw."

"Fuck, Evie, this isn't about the competition."

"Sure."

He runs a hand through his hair. "We were stupid. You were running hot and then cold. We didn't want to pressure you if you wanted an out."

"Got it. And the photos?"

"I did need pictures for the show, but I wouldn't use them without your permission. I swear. It's up to you, it was always up to you."

"Whatever. At least you got something out of this." I start

to close the door and he slips his fingers in the crack to stop it.

"Evie. We never meant to hurt you."

"I know. It was just a game."

"No, fuck it. You were the prize. Always. If you believe nothing else, believe that. You're the prize."

"Great. I'll put it on my Fetlife profile."

He sucks in a breath. "What do you mean—"

"Ask Bear. Goodbye, Sawyer." I walk away from the door. Eventually he'll leave.

You're the prize.

"Yeah, right," I mutter. If that's true, he wouldn't be leaving, and Bear wouldn't have already found my replacement.

A shout rings out on the lawn outside my apartment. I step onto the balcony in time to see Sawyer storm toward Bear.

"What the fuck, man?" Sawyer plants a hand on his friend's chest and pushes. Bear doesn't budge but Sawyer doesn't seem to notice. "Did you hurt her?"

A rumble from Bear—too low for me to hear his answer.

"You and your stupid kink," Sawyer shouts. "What did you do to her?"

Now they're fighting. Fuck. I did this.

Sawyer throws a punch. I'm out the door and dashing down the stairs. They're facing off on the lawn by the time I'm running towards them.

"Stop! Just stop!"

Sawyer backs off, jaw clenched. "We had one rule—don't hurt her. What did you do?"

"I don't know what this is about," Bear growls. "Evie?"

"It's no one's fault. I'm just done." Cool, calm, sophisticated. Act like your heart isn't bleeding out on the floor. "Thanks for the memories." I pause before I head back in. "You can use the photos." It's not like I'm going to leave my house anytime soon. I'll call my cousin with my regrets, and my boss to negotiate a work from home offer. I'll subsist on takeout and gain eight hundred pounds. They can lift me out with a crane when I die.

Halfway to my apartment, a large hand catches my arm. I halt but refuse to look up. "Let go."

"Talk to me," Bear orders.

"Too late. Too fucking late." I rip my arm out of his grasp. "You want to talk? Or do you want to fix me?"

"Evie—"

"I'm not a goddamn project. You, Sawyer, my aunt. What the hell is wrong with me? Why does everyone want to change me? I know I'm pathetic. Can you just leave me alone?"

"You're not a project."

"A competition then.

"Evie, I'm not playing a game." He slams his hand on the wall above my head. "It was never a game for me."

I stare at him, chest heaving. It hurts inside. It really, really hurts.

He catches my chin, gently. "It's not a game," he repeats and says something really scary. "It's real."

"And now it's over."

CHAPTER 8

I almost call Mina and ask how hard it would be to change my identity. Wipe Evangeline aka Evie off the face of the earth. Move to Paris. Take up smoking—that might help me lose weight. I'll be skinny but I'll still wear all black. Auntie Jen will approve.

I don't call Mina. I don't call anyone. I keep my head down, go to work, and pretend I'm an expatriate in a foreign country, with no ties to anyone.

I turn off my phone, which turns out to be a good thing, because Auntie Jen phones me nine hundred times the week before the wedding, volun-telling me to go pick up flowers, bridesmaids gifts, chocolate cupcakes with pink frosting. *Be sure not to sample, Evangeline! We got an exact amount*. Right up to the morning of the wedding, when she wanted me to fetch the tiara my cousin forgot at her apartment. I get none of these messages, and when I stick my head in to give my cousin my love before her walk down the aisle, my aunt nearly bites my head off.

I turn on my phone as I walk into the church, and, sure enough, it shakes to life and keeps vibrating alerting me of all the voicemails and texts I've missed. Nine hundred from Auntie Jen, one from my friend Mina, and one from Sawyer. "I'm sorry."

I search for something from Bear and find a big fat nothing.

Shaking my head, I stick my phone in my purse. I'm wearing the dress Bear chose for me. It's just a dress, right?

The two ushers—friends of the groom—fall over themselves to seat me. One of them is kinda cute. Maybe I can snag him before the reception and say he's my date. Wedding receptions are great places for singles to hook up, right? Or does that only work for bridesmaids?

I've just resigned myself to being a slutty bridesmaid-wannabe when my phone vibrates. Out of habit I pull it out.

"Where are you?"

"At the wedding. Why?"

"Turn around."

I do and make a noise like, "Uuunf." The guys are there, looking orgasmicly hot in tuxes.

"Wow," I say, before I remember I'm mad at them.

Sawyer grins. Bear is more impassive.

"You're here?" I want to ask. *"Why?"* But as I stare, I realize it was never a question of whether they were there for me when I needed them. Even if what we had was a bit of fun for both of them, they cared for me. And it's not like they made me any promises.

Carp. Okay, then. I can play nice, for the duration of a wedding. Better we don't make a scene. Or make a bigger scene than dowdy ole Evangeline showing up to her cousin's wedding with not one, but two gorgeous dates.

A pair of little old ladies pass Bear and rubber-neck, gawking at his giant frame. He looks out of place and larger than life, a bear at a tea party.

I offer a small smile as truce. I've missed them so much. Maybe we can be friends.

Sawyer steps forward to greet me.

"Evie," he kisses me on the cheek. "You okay?" He draws back, enjoying my admiring look. He poses in his tux. "You like these penguin suits?"

"I think they just made me pregnant."

He cracks up, and half the church turns to stare.

I flush bright red.

"Evangeline," Aunt Jen bustles up. "We need you to—oh, hello." Her harried look switches from angry to charming, just like that. Bad witch, good witch.

"Hello," Sawyer says with a smile that packs the charm of Chris Helmsworth, Chris Pratt, and Chris Evans rolled into one. It's quite something. "I'm Sawyer."

"Hi, Sawyer," Aunt Jen nods to him and then Bear. "Friends of our little Evangeline?"

"She prefers Evie," Bear corrects her. My aunt stares up at him, blinking. Her mascara encrusted lashes look like tiny shriveled spider's legs.

"We're not her friends," Sawyer says. "Well, not just her friends."

"We're her dates," Bear confirms.

"What, both of you?" Jen's head swings from one to the other, eyes wide.

"That's right," Sawyer says and offers his arm to me. "Shall we?"

"Let's." I take his arm, and Bear's and together we saunter away from my flabbergasted aunt.

Sawyer takes my hand. Bear takes the other. I hang on, hoping the ceiling doesn't open up with an angel choir singing "Evangeline is sinner." I'm surprised my red hair doesn't catch on fire.

The wedding procession begins, and things only get more surreal. We rise for the bride, and Bear towers over everyone. People look for the flower girl and their eyes catch on us. I hear my name and along a whispered gasp, "Two men!"

When we sit down, Bear's arm ends up around my shoulders.

"You're wearing the dress I bought," he murmurs.

I nod. I've done my hair up in a swirling 50s 'do. I look like I belong on the set of *Mad Men.* Turns out, it's a good look for me. A few of my relatives gape at my revealed form, and there are several guys who can't stop glancing at me, even during the vows. Bear angles his body a little, blocking me from view as he glares.

A little old lady in the pew in front of us peers through her glasses, her eyes magnified. Sawyer gives her a little wave and she scrambles to turn around and whisper loudly in her companion's ear. Sawyer squeezes my knee.

At the reception, I stand between two pillars of masculine strength, sipping champagne. Every once in a while, a great aunt or remote family member wanders by and I introduce my date. Both of them. Then Bear awes and Sawyer charms them while I drink more champagne. When it's time to throw rice, I'm loose enough to hug them both and whisper thank you.

"Evie—" Sawyer says, but Bear stops him.

"Not here."

They walk me to my car. I hang on to both of their arms. I'm not that tipsy, but if I glance down my cleavage gives me vertigo.

I stop before I reach my car. There's no way Bear will let me drive home. I turn expectantly. The two men standing behind me are so beautiful, my heart stops a moment before resuming its beat.

"It wasn't a game," Bear rumbles.

"I—What?"

"It wasn't just a game. I saw you, I wanted you."

"We both did," Sawyer broke in. "You were so adamant you didn't date; I came up with this scheme. We'd joked about doing this with a girl who was game, but this was serious. I'm sorry. I'm sorry if I hurt you."

My head is shaking no before I blurt, "You didn't. I had fun."

Bear leans over me and I look up at him.

"What now? Where do we go from here?"

"I want to keep seeing you," his hand bracelets my wrist, then runs up my arm, creating goosebumps.

"But what about your new relationship?"

"What?"

"The one on Fetlife," I say and blush.

"You're on Fetlife?"

"No." The blush advances. "My friend said you were looking for a long time and then changed your status."

"Yeah, baby. Stopped looking after I met you."

Oh.

"I want this to work," Bear looks straight in my eyes. I cling to him as the world tilts under my feet. "I want you any way I can have you. We don't have to do any of the rules or discipline or kinky stuff."

"No," I surprise myself. "I liked that. It was fun. I want it all."

Sawyer grins at us both. "I've got to go set up my show, but I'll be back. Maybe you'll come down and see it?"

"We both will," Bear confirms. He keeps his hand on my back as Sawyer bends down and kisses me.

I lean into his lips to the soundtrack of shocked gasps. When I straighten, a few old ladies are hustling away, mouths open and eyes round.

"Sounds good," I tell him and wave his Jeep off.

Bear hovers at my elbow, a giant James Bond. I have no idea where he found a tux in his size.

I pivot slowly, hearing the ending movie credits music start to play. Bear's hands close around my waist.

"So," I keep my voice as normal as I can. "Wanna play?"

~

Epilogue #1

"This is incredible," I tell Bear as he hands me a glass of champagne. As I spin on my heel, taking in the gallery full of Sawyer's photography, he keeps a hand at the small of my back. He's pretty possessive tonight. Not surprising, considering the final part of the exhibit are six pictures of me wearing nothing but freckles and salt spray.

A woman turns from examining a photo, sees me and does a double take.

"Is that...?" She points to me and the group turns to compare me to the black and white photos on the wall.

I sip my champagne, wishing the glass was bigger to hide the red in my cheeks. None of the pictures show more than a hint of my naughty bits, but with all the skin on display, they might as well. With the ragged bluffs behind me and the sand and surf curling around my naked body, I look like part of the landscape, my curves as timeless and epic as the rocky cliffs and sky.

I check the price tag, but the little cards all say "Private collection. Displayed with permission of the owner."

"I guess it's good that Sawyer sold something, but it's weird to think my bare ass is going to be hanging on some rich art collector's wall," I remark.

"Not happening," Bear growls. "I bought them all."

My mouth falls open. "Are you gonna display them?"

"Why would I?" He bends down to press his forehead against mine. "I've got the real thing."

I slide a hand along his cheek, angling my face for a kiss when a cocky voice breaks in.

"No, no, none of that please." Sawyer strides up, looking dashing in his tux. "At least, not while I don't have my camera." He winks at me.

I glance at Bear and he nods. With a happy cry, I throw myself into Sawyer's arms.

"I take it back," he laughs. "You can have all the PDA you want."

"That's a double standard," I tell him.

"It's a double something," he hugs me tight, pressing his dick against me before kissing my cheek. Throwing an arm around me, he turns me to my handsome date. "Well? You takin' care of my girl?"

"She's mine," Bear corrects. His eyes heat me.

People are staring but I don't care.

"Now, boys," I step between them, a hand on either chest. "There's enough of me to go around."

"Oh, so it's happening?" Sawyer asks. I don't understand but Bear nods, stepping close to claim me again.

"Tonight."

"What's this about?" I ask.

Bear turns me to him and dips his head. "We never had our final round."

Confusion flits over my face. His forehead meets mine, rocking gently.

"Not what you think. This isn't the end of us. It's the beginning. Sawyer and I want to do what we planned, to celebrate the end of the competition, and the start of something beautiful?"

"Yes," I reach up to twine my arms around his neck. "I'd like that."

Someone comes to ask Sawyer a question. Bear hands him a white keycard and gives him our room number before he turns away.

"Come on, baby." Bear takes my arm and steers me towards the exit.

"We're leaving already?"

"Not exactly," he pulls me into the private bathroom and locks the door. "Bend over the sink," he commands.

"Now?" I'm already turning.

"Now." He smacks my bottom and pulls my dress up over my hips.

I glance over my shoulder and he's got a bottle of lube and a butt plug.

"Seriously?"

"I gotta get you ready." He strips down my panties. "Lean forward, legs apart." His fingers delve into my cleft, spreading lube and probing my rear entrance. "Reach back and spread your cheeks." By the time he works the plug in, my pussy is dripping.

"There." He wipes away the excess lube, pulls up my panties and fixes my dress.

He makes me wear the plug through the rest of the exhibit and the ride back to the hotel.

By the time the doorknob to our room turns and Sawyer walks in, I'm desperate. "Fuck." He stops in his tracks.

I'm stretched over the bed, arms tied, and rear pointed towards the door. The butt plug winks at him from between my cheeks. "Evie," Sawyer murmurs, coming the rest of the way to trail his fingers over my ass.

"She's ready for you," Bear tells him. Bear's been teasing me with a vibrator and I'm wetter than I've ever been. "I've been training her, and she's done very well."

Sawyer's fingers on my skin still. "Does that mean—"

"You can take her ass if you want," Bear says to Sawyer magnanimously. It's so hot how he assumes ownership of my body. I squirm until Bear lays a hand on my back. "Be still, baby. You've done so well. Please Sawyer and you can come." He strokes my back as a second set of hands explores my naked body as if getting reacquainted. It's only been a week and a half since Sawyer left, but Bear has put me through my paces, making it clear how he feels about me. Boyfriend Bear, Bossy Bear, I've got it all.

"Evie," Sawyer bends down to meet my eyes. "Is this okay? Do you want this?"

"I do," I reassure him. "I've been looking forward to it." What I have with Bear is completely satisfying, but the thought of playing with both of them sends my libido into the red zone.

"And your ass?" Sawyer cups my rear. "Is it ready for me?"

"As ready as I'll ever be." I roll my eyes and he smacks my ass before massaging it.

"I don't know," he says, morphing into Stern Sawyer before my eyes. "I think it's not red enough for me."

"Yes, daddy," I murmur submissively and he fumbles with the fastener on his pants.

"Suck it. Make me feel good while I spank you."

I open my mouth and do just that, humming happily

around his cock as he smacks my upturned ass. In no time, he's ready, moving around to work the butt plug in and out of my bottom, admiring my stretched hole before pushing the plug back in.

"You want this?" he asks. I moan, nipples turned to diamonds.

"Yes, daddy, please—"

"Fuck," he mutters like a prayer for the second time tonight. The plug leaves my ass with a pop. He sets his cock at my gaping hole and pushes in. I wriggle, trying to get comfortable.

"Stroke her clit," Bear advises. "If you do, she'll come on your dick."

"Fuck, yes," Sawyer rocks gently in and out of my ass, his fingers finding my wet folds.

"Daddy?" I crane my head and Bear nods.

"You have permission to come."

I shiver. It's so natural and hot, how Bear takes control. Sawyer's finger finds the right spot and I make all sorts of needy noises.

"That's right, dirty girl," Sawyer mutters. "Give it to me. Come with my cock up your ass."

Tingles spread over my back, my orgasm making my pussy and asshole clench. Sawyer goes off on a cursing spree.

"Feel good?" Bear asks, amused.

"Her ass is milking my cock. Oh, fuck—"

A large hand on my neck makes me look up. Bear smiles at me, his bobbing cock filling my vision before sliding into my mouth. I suck and lick just the way he likes, the way he's taught me. The sight of us must send Sawyer over the edge, because he gasps and bangs out his climax. Once he pulls out, Bear flips me over and takes his place between my legs.

"Come as much as you want, beautiful," Bear says before sliding in and bringing me home.

"Was that enough for you, baby?" Sawyer asks later. I'm in the middle of the king bed in his arms with Bear at my back. Bear's letting me snuggle with Sawyer but I can sense him waiting to tug me into his arms before I fall asleep so he can spoon me.

"No," I smile. "I'll never get enough."

"Challenge accepted."

I shiver. Bear was right. This wasn't the end of the game.

This is the beginning.

Epilogue #2

"You look so beautiful," my cousin Genevieve breathes, pulling my veil down.

"So do you."

"Pssh," she waves a hand while the other rests on her belly. Her nice, round, pregnant belly. "This is your day." She takes my arm and turns me to the mirror. "Look at you."

"Look at you. You're glowing."

"So are you." We grin at our reflections. My cousin is willowy, I'm curvy, but we're both stunning. Why did I ever think it was a competition? There's enough beauty in the world for both of us. "Now go sit. I know your feet are killing you." Genevieve didn't want to be a bridesmaid, in case of early labor, but she insisted on helping me with as much of the wedding planning as possible while I was busy with my first tax season as an independent bookkeeper. "You did the same for me," she argued when I protested, and I gave up.

She actually enjoyed picking out the right shade of roses to match my blue wedding dress.

A few minutes later, I walk down the aisle towards the two gorgeous men waiting at the altar.

Bear and Sawyer straighten when they see me.

I smile at the blond before taking my spot facing Bear. My soon-to-be husband.

"So beautiful," he rumbles too low for anyone but me to hear. He pats his pocket, where recognizable blue lace peeks out. It's not a handkerchief. He totally didn't allow me to wear panties today.

My thighs clench and I have to remind myself that no one can tell. Not that people need a reason to judge. As we wait for the ceremony to start, I realize Auntie Jen snagged prime seating in the first pew.

"I heard she was dating both of them," she whispers to a blue-haired friend of hers. Her pinched expression says *slut!*

"Really?" the blue hair breathes. "Good for her." Blue hair cranes her neck to get a better look at my two men as the minister begins.

If only she knew. I'm with Bear now. His businesses were my first independent clients. Sawyer travels most of the year, selling enough photography to subsidize his surfing. Whenever he's back in town, we invite him to play a little game with us...

So, I'm not surprised at the reception dinner when Bear leans in close.

"I have a gift for you," he murmurs in my ear. "Sawyer's free tonight, if you want him to join us." He sits back and gives me a searching look.

I wet my lips. "May we...?"

"He can come play. As long as you remember you belong to me."

"Yes, daddy," I whisper. And as the crowd calls for our first dance, I follow Bear onto the floor, tucking my gorgeous curves against his giant frame. In my teetering heels, if I push up onto tiptoe and Bear leans down, I can just peek over his broad shoulder.

Sawyer's on the edge of the dance floor. I raise my brows and wink at him.

The camera flashes once before he lowers it and winks back.

Mini-shiver.

I snuggle against Bear. Two guys, one wedding night. I better eat extra cake 'cause I'm gonna need the calories.

Bear lifts his head when I chuckle.

"What is it, baby?"

"Remember our competition?"

"Yeah."

I lay my cheek against his to whisper in his ear, "I win."

The End

GET YOUR FREE BOOK!

You know you want it!

Royally Bad

Billionaire. Playboy. Prince. My new boss.

—>Bossy bad boy billionaire

—> Heroine who refuses to be intimidated

—>He's next in line for the throne...if he can keep his dick in his pants and name out of the tabloids

—> She's not falling in love with her arrogant, annoying, sex god boss. Nope. No way.

Grab it for free! https://BookHip.com/MQTSGH

ALSO BY LEE SAVINO

Contemporary Romance

Royal Bad Boy

I'm not falling in love with my arrogant, annoying, sex god boss. Nope. No way.

Royally Fake Fiancé

The Duke of New Arcadia has an image problem only a fiancé can fix. And I'm the lucky lady he's chosen to play Cinderella.

Beauty & The Lumberjacks

After this logging season, I'm giving up sex. For...reasons.

Her Marine Daddy

My hot Marine hero wants me to call him daddy...

Her Dueling Daddies

Two daddies are better than one.

Innocence: dark mafia romance with Stasia Black

I'm the king of the criminal underworld. I always get what I want. And she is my obsession.

Beauty's Beast: a dark romance with Stasia Black

Years ago, Daphne's father stole from me. Now it's time for her to pay her family's debt...with her body.

Paranormal romance

The Berserker Saga and Berserker Brides (menage werewolves)

These fierce warriors will stop at nothing to claim their mates.

Draekons (Dragons in Exile) with Lili Zander (menage alien dragons)

Crashed spaceship. Prison planet. Two big, hulking, bronzed aliens who turn into dragons. The best part? The dragons insist I'm their mate.

Bad Boy Alphas with Renee Rose (bad boy werewolves)

Never ever date a werewolf.

AUTHOR BIO

Lee Savino has plans to take over the world, but most days can't find her keys or her phone, so she just stays home and writes smexy (smart + sexy) romance. She loves chocolate, lives in yoga pants, and looks great in hats.

For tons of crazy fun, join her Goddess Group on Facebook or visit www.leesavino.com to sign up for her mailing list and get a free book.

Website: www.leesavino.com

Facebook: Goddess Group: https://www.facebook.com/groups/LeeSavino/

Created with Vellum

Manufactured by Amazon.ca
Bolton, ON